The Pict

The Pict

Jack Dixon

Standing Stone Press
USA

The Pict

Copyright © 2007 Jack Dixon

Standing Stone Press books may be ordered through booksellers or by contacting:

Standing Stone Press
www.standingstonepress.com

Standing Stone Press is an imprint of Ridley Park Books

Because of the dynamic nature of the Internet, any Web addresses or links contained in this book may have changed since publication and may no longer be valid.

This is a work of fiction. All of the characters, names, incidents, organizations, and dialogue in this novel are either the products of the author's imagination or are used fictitiously.

ISBN: 978-0-9817671-2-3 (pbk)
ISBN: 978-0-9817671-1-6 (cloth)
ISBN: 978-0-9817671-0-9 (ebk)

Second Edition, 2009

United States of America

For Karen

Pronunciation Guide – Pictish Names

Ailpein	AHL-pen		Fionnlagh	FIN-lah
Aodhan	AI-dan		Frangag	FRAN-gah
Baelagh	BAY-lah		Gabhran	gav-RAHN
Berchan	BAIR-khan		Giric	GEE-rig
Bhaltair	VAL-taar		Girom	GEE-rom
Boudiccea	BOO-di-ka		Liusaidh	LOO-sae
Brude	BROOD		Maerla	MAIR-la
Cailean	KAY-len		Melcon	MEL-kon
Cait	KATdh		Morbet	MOR-bit
Calach	KAH-lakh		Muthill	moot-ILL
Cirigh	KEE-rik		Nectan	NAY-tan
Cruithne	KRUN-yeh		Niall	NY-al
Diarmaid	DYAR-mit		Scoti	SKO-tee
Domhnall	DOM-nal		Selgovae	SEL-go-vay
Dubhgall	DOOV-gal		Sioltach	SHOL-takh
Dungal	DOON-gal		Smertae	SMAIR-tay
Eimhir	AY-ver		Suemas	SHAY-mus
Fidach	FEE-thah		Tearlach	TAIR-lach

1

Cruithne

THE BATTLE HAD BEEN RAGING for almost an hour before the sun broke the eastern horizon. The brutal Urnifal had attacked from the south without a warning while the Scythian village had barely begun to stir. It was the third attack in as many weeks.

The new light of the rising sun flashed across Cruithne's axe as he swung it ferociously into the chest of his maniacal attacker. The axe sank deep into the warrior's heart, and the warrior's expression transformed from twisted, seething fury into the shocked realization of his impending, inescapable death. The dying warrior dropped his mace and fell heavily to the dusty ground.

Cruithne turned from his fallen foe to survey the battle that raged around him. His people were fighting well and bravely, but they were far outnumbered by the aggressive Urnifal tribe. Cruithne knew that this battle would be yet one more devastating blow to his dwindling tribe, and that it would push them even farther toward the raging northern sea in search of refuge beyond the reach of the relentless Urnifal.

Cruithne knew that he must signal retreat. His warriors had once again bought enough time for the rest of the tribe to escape, but now it was time for the warriors to save themselves. He hoped that they would not take too many casualties in their escape. Without hesitation, he turned to shout the order, and word spread among his warriors to cede the field.

At Cruithne's signal, Fiedhan the horn blower raised his instrument to his lips to sound the call. Its unearthly sound echoed plaintively across the field.

Satisfied that his order had been relayed, Cruithne turned his attention from Fiedhan and back toward the battle. As he did so, the call to retreat was abruptly silenced.

Cruithne turned again to see Fiedhan hurtling backwards as an Urnifal spear impaled his throat. The spear stuck hard into the ground, and the weight of Fiedhan's body carried him along the spear's shaft and to the ground, nearly severing his head. Fiedhan was dead before he hit the ground, but not before his tribe had heard his call. The Scythians had begun their precarious withdrawal.

Cruithne turned to confront yet another attacker. He ducked his head, and narrowly dodged a heavy, spiked mace that would have easily crushed his skull. He lunged reflexively and swung hard, severing the arm that carried the mace. Both spun wildly away from Cruithne and his attacker. The Urnifal warrior grimaced, clutching his left hand over the remaining stump of his right, trying vainly to staunch the spurting blood. Cruithne buried his axe in the forehead beneath his enemy's horned helmet, and then he yanked it loose as searing pain shot through his back.

Cruithne saw the arrow protruding from his left side. It had entered from the back, tearing through the muscle below his armpit. He swore and grasped the shaft to break it off. He knew he had to end this battle without delay.

Cruithne led his warriors in the retreat, and to his great frustration they did suffer heavy casualties in the process. The Urnifal pursued the Scythians relentlessly, intent on killing every one of them before they escaped.

But Cruithne's tribe belonged to the fragmented remnants of a vast and long-indomitable tribe of equestrian archers. They were swift and agile, whether on foot or mounted on their smallish, nimble horses. Most of them escaped the innumerable but lumbering Urnifal, and within the hour their attackers had given up pursuit.

The decimated remnants of Cruithne's tribe fled north until they reached the shore of the icy, seething sea. The sea appeared to be endless and uninviting, and most of the refugees considered it an insurmountable obstacle to their escape. They made camp there on the shore, where a fierce wind blew dampness in from the sea, chilling them to their bones.

Cruithne looked across the open field as his people settled their families and their possessions for the night. Before long, most of them would gravitate toward the council fire at the center of the camp. Cruithne stood patiently, and waited. The tribe was pressed to decide on a plan that would allow them to survive, to heal, and to plot a course for whatever future might lay ahead.

Watching his small group settle in for the night, Cruithne vowed to do everything in his power, to give his life if necessary, to ensure that this struggling band endured.

It wasn't long before the council fire was ringed with solemn faces, glowing orange in the flickering firelight. The tribal tattoos etched into those faces seemed to shimmer and dance in the undulating glow.

Cruithne stood before them, looking grave. When enough had gathered, he began to speak to them of the challenge they faced.

"From the dawn of our time until now," Cruithne said, "for as long as we can remember, our people have never known slavery or defeat." Cruithne paused for a moment. "We have also never known peace."

Several around the fire nodded in agreement.

Fierce in battle and sworn to eternal independence, the one thing the Scythians valued more highly than peace was their freedom. But they had always longed for both. In these Indo-European steppes, however, the combination of peace and freedom was increasingly, maddeningly elusive.

"Through countless wars and fragile truces," he continued, "the endless pressure of raiders, pillagers, and now the builders of empires have worn us down. We are weak, and no longer able to survive in this land, standing against these hordes. The Urnifal will not stop until we are all dead, or driven into the sea."

Cruithne looked around at the solemn, forlorn, and fearful faces of his remaining tribesmen. Their sense of hopelessness was palpable.

"There's no more north to run to," said Fidach, one of Cruithne's seven sons, indicating the sea upon which they had come. "What is left for us to do?"

"West," replied Cait, with certainty. Cait was another of Cruithne's sons. "They're coming from the south and the east. We can only go west."

"If we move quickly," Fidach agreed, "as far to the west as possible, perhaps we will buy time to build boats, and take to the sea. These plains tribes won't follow to the sea."

Cruithne nodded thoughtfully. Many Scythian tribes had been able seafarers who had explored distant lands, bringing back wondrous goods and incredible tales. Cruithne's tribe included a handful of veterans of such voyages, and they told of vast tracts of land and islands to the west, which were less hospitable but far more isolated than were these open plains. Cruithne was willing to accept inhospitable isolation over the extermination of his tribe.

"The sea is too forbidding," Cirigh protested. "Most of us are unfamiliar with sailing. The sea could kill us all."

"The Urnifal *will* kill us all," Cait retorted. "Do you have a better plan?"

"Stay on the land," Cirigh replied, "and continue west."

"The land will limit our speed," Cruithne said, "and our enemies will pursue us on land. Fidach and Cait are right. The sea is our only hope. No one will dare pursue us beyond that." He indicated the rolling, crashing, wind-whipped sea. "We must take the chance."

The debate continued for some time, and through the night it evolved into planning. By the wee hours, in the darkness by the sea, the tribe reached a firm decision that would quickly lead to unwavering action.

The tribe, practiced hunters of the plains, effectively covered their trail, and took flight towards the west. Short nights and long days led the tattered clan farther from the reach, and just beyond the interest, of the Urnifal, who finally had possession of what they had long sought – the ancestral lands of the Scythian tribes.

After a week of urgent flight, and several more of anxious preparations, the band of weary refugees finally took to the icy sea in long boats filled with all that they could carry. They sailed to the west, fighting the waves and currents and cold. They were to lose most of their women and children along the way.

The Scythian voyagers chose to call their tribe Cruithne, in honor of their trusted, fearless leader. At that moment, the Scythian race was made extinct, its dwindling remnants spread along the fringes of what had once been their vast and fertile territory, replaced forever by the aggressive culture that had driven them out.

The Cruithne sailed for weeks. They landed at long last upon an empty rocky beach at the foot of a steep cliff that extended high into the clouds. It was not a welcoming place, but it was more inviting than the angry sea. They set camp and sent scouting parties to explore the land, hoping to find it both inhabitable and deserted.

A small expedition of the sturdiest of sailors continued the journey by sea to the west, hoping to find a more welcoming home. If they found one, they would return for the remainder, which stayed on the rocky coast to recover from the journey, and to explore. The elderly, the women, and the children that had survived the voyage were in poor condition and could go no farther.

The men that sailed west followed the coastline as it turned sharply south, and they eventually arrived upon the milder coast of another island to the west, across the sea from the mountainous island that they had been circumnavigating.

On the western island, they found beautiful land that was ripe for farming and settlement. But the island was already inhabited by a hearty and welcoming people. They were the "Scoti," they said, meaning "wanderers." It was an ancient name, of which they were very proud.

The Scoti were friendly, but they had strange ways. They welcomed the ragged travelers warmly and offered them food and drink. They bid them stay as long as they pleased, provided it wasn't too long, and asked them where they thought they might end up settling.

The visitors replied hopefully that they thought they might settle here, among the friendly Scoti, on this beautiful and welcoming western island.

The Scoti laughed kindly and long, and they added that they thought maybe not. They explained to their guests that they were open to having neighbors close by, but that they weren't interested in adding to their clan. It was a matter of pride, they said. They pointed back toward the northeast, saying that there was plenty of fine land back there, with more than enough room for settlers. The Scoti assured the Cruithne of their assistance should they meet with trouble.

The Cruithne explained to the Scoti that they had left most of their party back there on a rocky coast to the northeast, and that the land there didn't look at all hospitable. The Scoti advised them to surmount the imposing cliffs, where they would find in the highlands more suitable land. They might also encounter unsociable tribes, but the Scoti repeated their assurance of assistance if it were needed. The Scoti had often traded with a few tiny eastern highland tribes, and they insisted that they were relatively harmless. They offered to send a contingent of their tribe to help in the establishment of the Cruithne settlement. The Cruithne readily accepted the generous offer.

The Cruithne expedition worked out one last agreement with the Scoti. Since so few women and children had survived the journey, the Cruithne would need to take wives to ensure their survival. The Scoti agreed to the arrangement on one crucial condition. With cunning and long-range forethought, the Scoti insisted that the newcomers adopt a curious custom for that age: royalty and inheritance were to pass through the woman's bloodline in the event of the slightest disagreement.

The Cruithne were familiar with the notion of matrilineal inheritance, although its practice had all but disappeared from their culture centuries before. Women had always held the highest honor among their people. From the earliest days, the Scythians marveled at the miracle of childbirth, and regarded it as proof of the divinity of the female spirit. Women were the source of human life. Men viewed the power that women held over the continuation of life with wonder and admiration.

The Cruithne readily embraced the Scoti proposition, and the deal was struck. Scoti wives would ensure the survival of the newest arrivals to the sanctuary of the western islands.

In the world from which they came, this Scythian clan had long craved peace; in their new home, they vowed to make it their destiny. Over the ensuing centuries, peace and freedom became their creed, and they swore to defend one another to their last breath if necessary.

The Cruithne flourished and grew. In time the tribe split into seven distinct tribes, each headed by one of Cruithne's sons. Over the centuries, more tribal splits occurred, until there were twenty, covering the northern half of the island. Twelve tribes remained in the imposing highlands, and eight moved to the lowlands farther south.

Except for occasional skirmishes among the tribes, usually spurred by familial disputes, the Cruithne lived in relative peace. There were periodic forays into Cruithne lands by invaders from the east, but they always failed. The Cruithne were fiercely self-protective, and their adopted land was inhospitable and unforgiving to the outsiders. The Scoti, good to their word, assisted occasionally in repelling the invaders, but their involvement was rarely necessary. Cruithne determination was enough to ensure their success.

The Cruithne, long accustomed to hardship, grew comfortable with the harshness of the land and contentedly made it their home. Invasions subsided over time as the invaders lost their attraction for the difficult environment, and their patience with Pictish intractability. Over generations, the Cruithne adapted well, and they grew to regard their new home as temperate and comfortable. They desired no other place on earth.

2

Calach

THE YOUNG BOY KNELT at the edge of a precipice looking out over the mist-filled valley below. Storm clouds billowed and churned, and lightning bolts flashed within them, illuminating the heavy darkness of their depths. Calach smiled faintly as huge, cold raindrops pelted his fair skin, rolling down his face and dripping from his chin. Reddish-brown locks framed his face in damp curls, and flowed freely over his shoulders. His hazel eyes were sharp and alert, taking in every detail of his world.

Young Calach loved this land. He loved the power and the strength of it, and the pride with which it filled his heart. As he surveyed the highland home of his hearty tribe, a fierce determination gleamed in his eyes, and he drew back his shoulders, filling his lungs with its sweet fragrance.

Calach knew all the myths and stories of old. He could recite them from memory, just as he had heard them from his first days. He spent hours at a time here in his secret place, meditating and thinking of his ancestors who had come here so long ago, from a far off Eastern place

that existed only in a thousand-year-old myth. There were tales of
extreme brutality and endless war, tribes in eternal conflict over hunting
and territory and gods, each tribe fighting to control and to subdue all
others, and to ensure its own survival. And in the end all were overcome
by the ravenous Urnifal horde from the east.

The ancient engravings on an ageless standing stone to Calach's
right, near the edge of the clearing, told the historic tale. An ancient
artist had etched pictograms of the journey below the deeply carved
symbol of the Cruithne clan – two circles side by side, connected by two
curved lines, which were in turn bisected by the median line of a
superimposed z-rod. Below the z-rod symbol, several long ships fought
the sea. Below the ships, several figures clasped hands. The last symbol,
at the bottom of the stone, almost hidden by thriving straw grass, was a
classic depiction of the spirit of Cruithne himself – an inverted crescent
superimposed by an intersecting v-rod. Calach examined the standing
stone with admiration and respect. He contemplated the lives that had
passed since the stone was first carved and erected.

When Calach's people arrived at this land they called themselves
Cruithne, a name that the Scoti also came to call them, after their
leader. Over time they adopted the new name, "Pict," from an ancient
Scoti word that meant "fierce warrior."

Calach fancied himself the embodiment – perhaps the *reincarnation*
– of the man called Cruithne, the first hero and the greatest king of his
tribe. He tended and nurtured within himself the qualities he imagined
that Cruithne had certainly possessed, and with which he believed he
had been endowed by Cruithne's spirit at his birth: loyalty, strength,
wisdom, and honor.

Calach's deep kinship with his ancient hero strengthened over time,
until he was certain that he was indeed Cruithne reborn. The Picts
toyed with the idea of spiritual rebirth through reincarnation, though no
one claimed to understand fully the nature or the purpose of such a
thing. Calach was certain of its veracity, if not its workings.

To Calach it could not be clearer. He believed that he had been born to continue in Cruithne's footsteps, to devote his life to leading the Picts, and to protect them from outside interference or conquest. His mission was to make sure that this land remained the haven that it had always been for the Picts.

To Calach, there was nothing more comforting than this land. To him, its harshness was a cloak of protection for his people against trespassers and invaders. He found comfort in his own ability to tolerate its climate, and he was proud of his clan's success in melding into the fine tapestry of this beautiful place.

Calach wondered, though, how long it would be before the outside world turned to encroach upon, and to seriously threaten the Cruithne world. He wondered if the Urnifal would ever take up their trail and follow them here.

He was aware of stories and fables of distant lands, where violence and barbarism still thrived and raged. He knew that the world beyond his land was filled with voracious warriors that might someday come again to try to conquer and enslave his people.

And he knew of the Romans, who over the past few hundred years had forged a great empire over most of the world, including Pretani lands not far to the south, and who were still far from satiated by their relentless and widespread conquest.

Lightning cracked through the clouds overhead, wrenching Calach from his ponderous thoughts. The thunder rumbling through the valley reverberated through his bones and made his scalp tingle. He smiled to himself grimly and thought, *Let them come, whoever they are, and try to enslave my people. Let them come to face me.*

Calach's face hardened. He knew that if his people were attacked he would summon all of his strength, and call down the fiercest of his gods to fight by his side, and no one would ever enslave his people as long as Calach, the warrior boy, the reincarnation of Cruithne lived.

3

Girom

CALACH'S REVERIE DRIFTED through the afternoon as he sat gazing out over the valley. The descending sun finally broke through the clouds, and it began to warm his face. Its brilliance highlighted the many shades of green, amber, and orange that splashed across the vast valley, dotted by plentiful patches of purplish thorny thistle.

Somewhere in the distance, far across the valley, a piper began to play a soulful song, the haunting sound of his pipes drifting like the voices of spirits moving through and over the land. The soft pounding of a goatskin drum joined the moaning of the pipe, and the chorus they formed seemed to touch the very depths of Calach's soul.

Calach sat listening in the hollow of a huge, ancient oak in the center of the clearing of the ridge, contented in his thoughts, pleased by the sound, but considering that it was time to go home.

As he arose, he sensed a presence behind him. He heard the rustling of leaves and soft footsteps on the damp sod. He froze, alert.

"Is the young man enjoying the mountains' song?" The voice was gravelly and old, but soft. "What do you see out there, boy? What is it that you seek?"

Calach rose and turned to face the old man, who waved a spindly arm across the expanse of the valley. His leathery skin was bluish, and it bore numerous tattooed Pictish beasts and geometric symbols. Long, scraggly hair hung gray around his face, and over his scarred and sinewy shoulders. Old but muscular and heavily tattooed arms hung at his sides.

Calach regarded the old man with suspicion.

"Who are you?" he asked, in a steady voice. He stared intently at the old man.

The man sniffed, tilted his head back slightly, and gave Calach an odd sort of grin.

"No fear in you. Suspicion, but not fear. That's good. Your heart shan't ever know fear." It was a pronouncement. There was a distant, musical quality to the man's voice, and his eyes flashed like diamonds. "You are Calach, no?"

"Aye, Calach." Calach wondered how the old man knew his name.

"I know you well," the old man said, as if he were reading Calach's mind. "You come here often to these secluded hills. Why is it that you come here, lad? What do you seek?"

"It's peaceful here," Calach said curtly. He was slightly annoyed. The man still hadn't told him who he was. There was something oddly familiar about the man, but Calach was sure he'd never seen him before. "I asked you your name."

"Patience, lad. There's no need for menacing toward me. I'm no harm to you. Of that you can be sure. I only want a word with you, and maybe several back from you."

Calach remained quiet. He felt a strange, warm comfort in the old man's presence. And he was curious about the manner in which he spoke, as if he were from some other time...perhaps Cruithne's time.

"My name is Girom. This is my home." Girom waved his hand once more across the vista, as if indicating that it was *all* his domain.

"This place was sacred to your father's fathers, since long before your days. It has always been a secret place of meditation and prayer. I suspect you come here because your bones lead you here, and something in your blood. You come here seeking the spirit of your fathers, do you not?"

Calach's eyes narrowed as he regarded the man. He wondered how long, and how often, he had watched him from the shadows.

Calach did spend most of his time here on the craggy ridge thinking deeply about his family, his clan, and where they came from. He pondered the nature of his life, and its purpose. He sought answers and guidance, and confirmation of his suspicion that he was Cruithne, born anew for a purpose as yet undiscovered.

He hesitated to voice his thoughts about that, even to those who were closest to him. While he felt that it was the spirit of Cruithne that called him here, he did not want to say such a thing to this stranger. And yet, he felt compelled to do just that.

Girom stepped forward to stand beside Calach. He gazed down at the boy for a moment, and then he turned his eyes toward the vast expanse before them. He placed a hand on Calach's shoulder and heaved a heavy sigh. As he exhaled, his breath echoed in a strange moan that seemed to waft across the valley. In its moan, Calach thought he heard a barely intelligible, whispered word.

Cruithne, it seemed to moan softly.

Calach looked at Girom, startled by the sound.

Girom waved his hand across the sight of the valley below them once more, and he said, "Tell me, young Calach, what you see."

Calach looked away from Girom, and back across the valley. He considered the question for a long while, mulling it over and searching for the answer in his heart. He thought of the power he felt here, and the solace, and the peace. He considered his countless private thoughts and feelings, and tried to fuse them into one brief summary for old Girom.

"Everything worth seeing," he finally replied. "I see everything here that there is to see." Girom raised his eyebrows, questioning, but with the hint of a knowing smile.

"Do you think you might narrow that down a bit?"

"I see my people here, in their past, and how they live today. And I sometimes think I can even see...their future."

"Their future?" Girom raised his eyebrows yet further, and then he smiled and nodded appreciatively.

"I see the spirits of my ancestors here, and I see our gods here, too," Calach offered. "I see one spirit most clearly, and I sometimes think he speaks to me."

Girom listened quietly. Calach searched Girom's face to measure his reaction to the words, to no avail. Girom did not seem surprised. Calach turned his gaze back toward the landscape.

"I think our gods live here," he continued.

"Our gods?" Girom appeared to be mildly surprised by this.

"Our gods. As one. And maybe a king of gods. If there were a king of all the gods, the god-king would live here, I think. This is the land of the god-king." Calach paused to consider his own words. "I would be honored that the god-king has let me into his world, and let me call it my own. I wonder if there might really be such a god-king, Girom," Calach mused.

"I wonder," Girom grinned. "These are such big words for such a young boy. Your heart is strong, and open."

"And I see Cruithne here," Calach finally ventured, with mustered resolution. He cast a sideways glance at Girom, who locked eyes with him. "And I *feel* Cruithne," he said, placing his hand over his own heart, "*here*."

The two gazed at one another in silence for a moment, and then Girom nodded slowly, as if wordlessly affirming Calach's thoughts.

Calach continued. "I come here to honor my ancestors. I come here to honor our gods. Most of all," Calach said, almost in a whisper, "I come here to honor...and to find...Cruithne. I seek his wisdom, and his strength."

The thoughts and theories that Calach had long entertained in his solitude had begun to crystallize in his mind, and he somehow felt freer to express his innermost thoughts. He was beginning to see things in a way that really made sense to him, and somehow Girom's presence was helping to make that so.

"You may think me lost in the mist, Girom, but as sure as I sit here talking to you now, I have memories that seem...quite strange."

"Memories? Strange, how?"

"Memories...of standing in a ship, of sailing over a rough and icy sea, of urging worn and frightened people to survive. I am leading them, strengthening them, trying to give them the courage to go on, just a little longer, just a little farther."

"Cruithne," Girom nodded. Calach returned the nod.

"Leading them to the safety of this place," Calach added. "I even remember standing on the shore, relieved that we had come upon it not a moment too soon. I was overwhelmed by the sheer height of the cliffs, but I suspected there was something magnificent beyond them. I watched the expedition I had sent to sail off to the west, and I remember their return with the Scoti."

"You were told of these things as a boy, were you not?" Girom asked.

"I was," Calach agreed. "But never in such detail, and it always seemed more of a reminder than a revelation. It always felt like memories."

"Memories indeed," Girom said, to Calach's questioning eyes. After a pause, he continued. "Perhaps you are only imagining the history of your people. But then, memories they may very well be. Your connection is very strong. If yours is indeed the very spirit of Cruithne, then memories they may well be."

"The memories seem so real," Calach said.

Girom nodded, and then asked, "What do you think Cruithne carried in his heart at the end of his days so long ago, having seen his people pushed from their land, at the brink of extinction, into a perilous journey across unknown seas, to seek refuge in an unknown land?"

Calach pondered the question. He knew the answer, because he felt it in his heart, but he had to put it into words.

"Love for his clan," Calach began. "Commitment to their welfare."

"What else?" Girom prodded.

"Anger. Bitterness."

"Rage?" Girom asked.

Calach nodded vigorously.

"Rage," he firmly agreed.

The two sat quietly for a moment.

"Against what?" Girom finally asked. Calach looked perplexed by the question. He thought the answer obvious.

"The Urnifal. Fate. The thievery of Cruithne land, and the desolation of their people."

"Did the Urnifal do anything that is not in the nature of man to do?" Girom asked. Calach thought for a moment, cocking his head to the side as he considered the question.

"No," he said, hesitantly.

"They did, in fact, exactly what it is man's nature to do, did they not?" Girom asked.

"I suppose so. What is in the nature of *most* men, anyway," Calach replied.

"Then it was against man's very nature that Cruithne raged, and nothing else, was it not?" Girom sat back and looked full into Calach's eyes as Calach wrestled with the idea.

"It would seem so," Calach finally answered.

"What does one gain bearing rage against such inevitable things?" Girom asked. "Would not such rage be better put aside, to make room for better things, more constructive things?"

Calach nodded almost imperceptibly.

"And yet, you carry it still. Even into this life, you carry it still." Girom's eyes showed compassion as he gazed upon the boy.

"I...I do," Calach admitted.

"You rage against injustice wherever you think you see it. You rage against invaders who have not yet arrived. You rage against the future in the same way you rage against the past. And yet you say you do not feel rage."

"I didn't realize that I did," Calach said, "until you put your words so."

Girom smiled.

"Ah," said Girom. "So now we come to *my* purpose. It is this: I am to tell you something which I was asked long ago, before the beginning of your time, to come and tell you now. It is time for you to hear, and to consider, my words.

"You have come into the world in a purposeful place, and at a purposeful time. You have carried into the world the same burden that you carried when you last left it. Cruithne left this world with rage in his heart. You have carried that same rage back with you."

Calach listened carefully to Girom's words.

"You must take care," Girom warned. "You must overcome this rage. Such rage can only do you harm. It will trip you, and you will fall. It will blind you, and you will swing your sword in darkness, striking nothing."

"So I am to swing my sword, then," Calach said. "Against whom?"

"Against a tempest the likes of which your people have not seen in over a thousand years. Against the tempest that is brewing just beyond the horizon, to the south. You feel it brewing, and you know that it will come. You have long known, somewhere deep within you, that it would come."

Calach's eyes grew wide at Girom's words.

"Then I will swing my sword with rage," Calach said firmly.

Girom shook his head sadly.

"You have not listened."

Calach began to protest, but Girom continued, with a grave look.

"Rage simmers hotly in your heart, just beneath the surface. But the world is already filled with rage, Calach, and rage will turn out to be your biggest enemy. It will be a bigger challenge than any other you could conjure."

"I should think that in battle rage is justified, and useful," Calach argued.

"In battle, rage is blinding," Girom repeated. "Rage is weakness, born of fear."

"I do not know fear," Calach boasted.

"You may indeed never know what it is to be afraid. But you will most certainly come to know fear, to see it clearly in other men. Fear alone causes men to attack, to destroy, and to enslave others. Fear causes men to lose strength, reject honor, and to embrace the animal instinct to dominate. Men of fear would steal your freedom, destroy your peace, sap your strength, and challenge your principles. They will tempt you to become like them."

"I will never be afraid," Calach insisted. "I will never be like them."

"Then beware your rage," Girom said, his voice rising slightly. "Hear me well: rage, like all weakness, is born of fear. When you feel rage, know that you have become as weak as they are, and know that fear has taken you."

"Never," Calach said through clenched teeth.

"You will know that you have become weak when you are motivated by rage or vengeance. Fear will have claimed you when you hunger for your enemy's blood, and find pleasure in its taste. If that day comes, know then that lesser men have defeated you, and imparted to you the very fear that diminished them. If you should embrace hatred and rage, then know that you have lost much."

Calach nodded slowly, then, and thoughtfully. Girom's face softened as he saw that Calach was finally listening to him, and heeding his words. He placed a gentle hand upon Calach's head, and playfully tousled his hair.

"Not every soul chooses so noble a path as yours, my dearest Calach. Occasionally, one like you chooses a path that brings them in harm's way, close to evil and in the presence of fear. You must steel yourself for the journey that you have chosen, and do not stray from your path."

Calach looked up at old Girom with resolute eyes. He sensed that it would be a very long time before he would see Girom again, but somehow he knew that he would. He tried to absorb the fire in Girom's eyes, and to memorize each line in his weathered face. Girom's skin bore the marks and the bluish hue of Calach's Pictish people, and his words seemed to encompass their ancient wisdom.

The power of Girom's words imparted to Calach a feeling, a passion that filled his heart with strength, and certainty, and resolve. He vowed then to carry those things with him through all of his days.

4

Killing

CALACH WALKED CONFIDENTLY, purposefully, across the town square of Muthill. Muthill was his home, and the ancestral village of his clan. The village was located at the center of the Caledonii lands. The name of the town held deep meaning, not only for the Caledonii, but also for all of the Cruithne through the ages.

Muthill was a place of truce for the Cruithne tribes. The name itself conveyed peace and tranquility. Tribal leaders met here to discuss differences, negotiate agreements, and decide on matters of war and peace. Muthill was also the home village of every Caledonii king.

Calach was nearly twelve, nearly old enough for the hunt, and anxious for the day of his passage rite to arrive. He was happiest when he was wandering the fields and valleys of his tribal lands, scouting hidden trails and hunting small game. He had become quite adept at both hunting and scouting under the patient tutelage of Tearlach, his proud and powerful father.

He walked with his head held high, and with the blood of three dead rabbits trickling warmly between his shoulder blades. Some of the adults stopped what they were doing to watch him come in from his hunt, most smiling appreciatively at his catch, and more than a few with looks of curiosity. Calach was aware that many of his tribe thought him odd, and that some were wary of his unsettling introversion.

Calach nodded curtly toward almost everyone he saw. For a few select elders, however, he reserved a trademark respectful bow. He acknowledged almost everyone he saw, at least at some level, yet he was one of the quietest boys that anyone had ever known.

It was rare that Calach spoke with anyone at any length, for he never had much to say, and he was rarely comfortable saying it when he did. He often believed that if people came to know his thoughts, they would think him stranger still, and so he kept those thoughts to himself.

When he was a small boy, Calach's silence was the talk of his village. Some people speculated that he might grow to be entirely mute, or to disconnect with the world entirely, and turn insane. Almost everyone considered his strange introversion an impairment of his ability to deal with their untamed world. Some people simply thought him dense, and destined to be little more than a liability to anyone who was burdened with his care. Calach was aware of all the whispering and worrying, but he shrugged it off, having more important things to think about.

Calach also knew that his parents were wise, and that they knew better, even though they didn't fully comprehend his nature.

His father, Tearlach, had followed Calach in curiosity one summer day, as he wandered alone into the woods long before dawn. Calach was absorbed in his own world, apparently oblivious to the one through which he walked.

Tearlach maintained a discreet distance, sufficient to stalk a red deer stag across an open moor. He seemed confident that Calach would not detect his presence. He followed Calach until they reached the craggy cliff edge overlooking the magical, misty valley.

Tearlach knew this place to be one of historic refuge for many of his ancient ancestors. Myths had been handed down through the years about the wisdom and the inner strength that one could find here, if they wished it. Tearlach had only been to this place once or twice, as a child long ago, with his father when troubles had challenged their clan. The spirits were strong here, his father had solemnly proclaimed. He had bid Tearlach quiet as he sat in deep contemplation, and spiritual communion.

Tearlach sat now and watched his own son, in silence, for the better part of the day. Calach sat motionless, sometimes gazing into the expanse of the misty valley, and occasionally closing his eyes for long periods of prayer or meditation.

Toward late afternoon, Calach stood and stretched his lanky limbs. He turned to look intently toward the spirits with which he had communed, and he nodded in acknowledgement of their counsel. He walked to the edge of the precipice for one last, long look at the beautiful valley.

Tearlach turned and left quickly, as quietly as possible to avoid Calach's detection, and he hurried to reach the village long ahead of Calach.

Tearlach told his wife breathlessly when he'd returned, all that he could tell her of Calach's day. He marveled at Calach's comfort in the solitude of the ridge. Eimhir smiled quietly at the telling, and her heart filled with the pride of a mother who knew great and wonderful things about her son.

Later that evening, Calach sat with his parents around the crackling hearth of their modest home. Gabhran, Calach's beloved older brother, was away on a three-day hunt into the highlands. The fire was sputtering sporadically, in need of fresh logs.

Tearlach rose from the table and nodded toward his wife, who smiled warmly back. Calach watched Tearlach leave, and he listened as his footsteps retreated toward the woodpile. When he knew that his father was far enough off, he turned to his mother with a serious look.

"Why did father follow me today?" he quietly asked.

Eimhir started in surprise, her eyes wide.

"You saw him, then?" she asked.

"I felt him," Calach said. "I sensed his presence. I knew that he was near. I looked to see him from the corner of my eye, but I could not catch sight of him." Calach thought for a moment and smiled. "He's a fine hunter," he said, with pride.

"Aye, a fine hunter, indeed." Eimhir agreed. "And a good father, as well?"

"None could be better," Calach said. "Was he afraid for me?"

"Not afraid," Eimhir said. "Curious, yes. But not afraid. He wanted to know where you go, and why you go there. He's still wondering at it a bit, but he's a quick one to understand."

"That's good," Calach said. "And you understand?"

Eimhir nodded softly, reassuringly, as Tearlach reentered the house, his arms laden with heavy logs. He had caught the end of the conversation, and he shot Eimhir a questioning look. She deflected the look with a warm and loving smile, rushing to him to relieve his burden.

Calach's parents accepted that the depth of his spirit surpassed their ability to comprehend, or explain. Therefore, they didn't ever try. They allowed others to think what they would, and to form assumptions about their son's peculiarities, unanswered.

Calach continued his confident stride across the village square, the rabbits swinging from his shoulders as he walked. He saw Frangag, an older widow whose husband had been killed years earlier in a clash with Pretani raiders from the south, and he approached her with a grin.

Frangag flashed her crooked, toothless smile at Calach, and she reached out to tousle his wild hair. Calach bowed deeply, and then he reached back for one of his rabbits. It was still warm in his hand as he held it out toward Frangag.

"I got an extra one today," Calach said, as if it were different from any other day he brought rabbits from the fields. "Take this one. It's for you."

Frangag returned Calach's bow, and then she took the rabbit from his outstretched hand. Calach winked at Frangag, and then he turned on his heels toward home.

Frangag watched after him, nodding appreciatively.

Calach spied Gabhran a distance away. Gabhran was pushing and shoving in a mock battle with a group of his friends. Calach liked most of Gabhran's friends, but he thought that some of them were leeches, bound to him by the respect and admiration that Gabhran commanded among the tribe.

Calach made his way toward them now. He was eager to show Gabhran the fine, fat rabbits he had caught, so that Gabhran would look forward to their evening dinner.

Gabhran grinned widely at the sight of his younger brother. He shoved his friend Giric roughly to the side and took several steps toward Calach. Giric lurched headlong into a tree trunk, but Gabhran paid him no mind, opening his arms toward Calach.

"How goes it, brother?" Gabhran called out, still grinning. Giric, recovered from his stumble, had turned to rush Gabhran from behind. Calach called out a warning to his brother, but without waiting, he threw the rabbits to the ground and lunged toward Giric. Giric was one of Gabhran's friends for whom Calach harbored resentment.

Giric outweighed Calach by easily a third, but the force of Calach's momentum drove him backward into the same tree from which he had just recovered. Giric's body glanced off of the tree trunk and landed prone on the soggy ground.

In a flash, Calach sat astride Giric's shoulders, pounding his fists relentlessly into his face. Giric flailed wildly, occasionally connecting forcefully with Calach's crimson, contorted face. Calach didn't seem to notice the blows.

Calach had carried the memory of some offense that Giric had committed against his brother long ago. While Gabhran and Giric had long forgotten the conflict, and had since grown to become fast friends, the memory of it still burned in Calach's mind. He had sworn to avenge Giric's wrong. Seeing Giric coming at his brother from behind had reawakened that ancient vow. The memory of it had overtaken Calach's senses.

Gabhran fought to hold his other friends off as they moved to swarm his younger brother in Giric's defense. After several kicks to Calach's ribs, Gabhran's friends complied with his pleas. Gabhran himself pulled Calach off of Giric by the sash around his waist. Calach sputtered and flung his fists into the empty air while Gabhran pulled him away from the crowd.

"What's the matter with you, Calach?" he shouted. "What has gotten into you?"

"He hurt you," Calach barked, heaving heavily. "He was going to hurt you again!"

"What? He's my friend. We were playing! What do you mean, he hurt me? How did he hurt me?"

Giric stood now, glaring at Calach, blood streaming from his battered nose. His friends brushed the dirt from him, and consoled him, while restraining him from going after Calach.

"Don't you remember?" Calach cried, not believing that Gabhran had forgotten. "He hit you with a rock, from behind. He nearly knocked you unconscious, for no reason! I can't believe you don't remember!"

"Oh, ho, ho," Gabhran laughed, suddenly remembering the incident. He retrieved Calach's rabbits and threw his arm tightly around Calach's shoulders, guiding him forcibly toward home. "So you remember that? What a long memory you have! That was over three years ago!"

"So what," Calach insisted. "He hurt you, just the same."

"Only because I pushed his sister into the bog, face first," Gabhran explained. "I deserved that rock, Calach."

Calach looked at Gabhran in surprise. He had not imagined his brother could have deserved the blow.

"And besides," Gabhran continued, "he has become one of my closest friends. You should not have attacked him, you lunatic." Gabhran shook his head, incredulously. "I have to admit, though, brother...you certainly got the best of him there."

Gabhran looked at his brother with a mixture of pride and concern.

"I will say this, you crazy boy: you'll surely make a fine warrior one day, and one day not far off!" He tousled Calach's hair playfully, and then squeezed his shoulders tightly with affection. "Just try not to let your keen sense of justice get the best of you, little brother."

As the brothers walked toward home, Calach's eyes met with those of a girl his age. She stood watching them shyly from where she stood by the corner of her family's house.

Maerla's dark hair and wide, cerulean blue eyes were strikingly beautiful. She was coy and mysterious, and Calach was entirely captivated by her smile. Calach believed that he had successfully concealed his attraction for her, and his smile toward her was casual and reserved. His skin tingled when she returned his smile with a broad and pleasant one of her own, which seemed to illuminate her face.

Calach looked quickly away, cursing his inexplicable timidity. *I know no fear,* he railed at himself. *Why am I so shy around her?* Gabhran tactfully masked his awareness, and he acted as though he had not noticed Maerla at all, standing there in the shadows of her house.

Maerla haunted Calach's thoughts and dreams. At night he would close his eyes, and they would be filled with the image of her shy and pleasing smile. He vowed each night that one day he would take the action that would bring her into his life. The nature of the action that could accomplish that goal eluded him.

Fate has a way of working such things out.

Weeks later, autumn's chill was creeping in from the north, a little farther and a little colder with each passing day. Organized hunts had increased in earnest to lay up stores of meat for the winter. Calach longed to join the hunting parties, to prove his skills and show that he was grown. But he watched in frustration as each hunting party eagerly departed, and he watched in envy when each returned in triumph with its fresh kill. He was always left behind in the company of others his age, with whom he could find nothing in common, except for an occasional conflict or violent clash.

One dismal morning, Calach moped through the forest grumbling to himself about his plight. He carried his hunting bow, and the gutting knife he hoped he would get to use, should he stumble upon a prize stag of his own.

The sound of raucous laughter reached his ears, and Calach frowned in repugnance at the thought of encountering a boisterous group of boys from the village. He turned to move away from the sound, but he was stopped by a plaintive cry from among the shouts. Something was amiss. He stood quietly with his ears tuned to the sound.

He heard it again, a shrill cry piercing the antagonistic laughter. Someone, obviously a girl, was being harassed, or something worse. He turned back and moved quickly toward the sound.

Calach flew through the brush as nimbly and almost as quickly as any stag. Even with his bow across his back, and his dagger in his belt, he was virtually noiseless in his flight. Within minutes, he had crested a craggy ridge. He looked down with indignation upon a sickening scene below.

His eyes were first drawn to Maerla, at the center of a group of Caledonii boys. There were four of them, and they pushed Maerla from one to the next, grabbing at her, and laughing at her in insolent mockery.

Calach recognized the boys as some of the most unruly of the tribe. Berchan was the ringleader, a village bully. The other three were followers, ordinary troublemakers who followed Berchan for his notoriety, some measure of which they longed to claim for themselves. This group was well known for mischief and torment, and Calach loathed each of them.

Even the ancient Frangag had once suffered the oppression of Berchan and his friends, as they terrorized her without mercy one day at a distant edge of the village. They had suffered severe discipline for their misdeed against Frangag, but upon most of them the discipline had had little effect.

The sight of Maerla's torment enraged Calach. When Berchan, whom Calach detested most, pushed Maerla to the ground beneath him, Calach let loose his wrath. He deftly strung and arrow and let it fly. The arrow sang through the trees and landed with stunning precision, piercing the foot of one of the laughing spectators, and burying itself deeply into the soft ground beneath the boy's foot. Suemas's laughter escalated into a piercing, agonized cry.

Suemas's scream of agony was nearly drowned out by Calach's bellow of rage. Calach crashed like a madman through the brush down the hill toward the boys, his bow in his left hand and his dagger held firmly in his right. The boys looked up in dismay as Berchan pushed himself up and away from Maerla's flailing, disheveled body.

Calach had painted his body in the manner of a warrior bound for battle. He often did so when he set out on solo ventures into the forests. The sight of him now filled the four boys below him with panic and utter dismay. Two of them involuntarily turned to flee, but Berchan barked an order that froze them in their tracks.

Berchan reached into his sash and removed his own short dagger. The dagger was old and tarnished, having been given only shoddy attention over many years. Berchan's father had given it to him more as a plaything than as a weapon of war.

Calach's dagger was superior, long and shiny and sharp, and worthy of any of the most accomplished of Caledonii warriors. The fine, gleaming weapon had been handed down through generations of Calach's family by the man who had made it with his own hands. It had been given meticulous care, with great pride, by each of its successive owners.

Berchan noted the dagger, and the fury of Calach's approach. He was not prepared for this development. He had chosen a harmless target for his self-indulgence, and he had not planned to engage in any real confrontation. But he would rise to the inconvenient threat of this foolish intruder. He was all too conscious of his own infamy, of which he was proud, and which he was compelled to protect.

Berchan squared off to meet Calach's attack. He commanded his cohorts to stand fast in ready reserve. Calach descended on them and came to a skittering halt in front of Berchan, his eyes aflame with his rage. Suemas's foot remained firmly impaled to the ground, but the other two boys stood close behind Berchan.

Maerla scrambled frantically away from the boys, through a thistle patch that lay between her and the refuge of a thick oak. The searing pain of the thistle thorns that tore her palms and pierced her knees barely registered through the panic of her retreat. Her wide, beautiful eyes were filled with fear, and fixed upon her unexpected defender.

Calach glared into the depths of Berchan's eyes, and his intensity unsettled the brutish bully. Berchan waved his pathetic dagger in front of him, as if to ward off Calach's anger.

Calach stood firmly. He shifted his glare to each of the others in turn, and each of them stepped backwards in reflexive retreat. Berchan glanced at them, to either side, in disgust.

"Fool," Berchan growled. "Are you suicidal? You alone challenge all of us? We'll leave you both here to rot. No one will ever know your fate."

They were far enough away from the village that Berchan could have been right about that, but it mattered little to Calach just then.

"Back away," Calach warned.

"Or what?" Berchan demanded.

"Back away," Calach repeated. "Don't do this. You will regret it."

Berchan laughed derisively. The others joined in.

"Look at you, the warrior boy, all painted up for war," Berchan mocked. "You want a war? You have one." Berchan began to close in on Calach. The other boys closed in behind him, and Calach searched for his next move. He suddenly saw it.

Suemas moaned loudly, trying desperately to wrench his foot free. Dubhgall and Lachlan turned toward Suemas, distracted. Calach lunged and rolled across the ground, grasping a stout branch in the process, and springing quickly to his feet behind the two distracted boys.

Calach brought the branch down solidly on the crown of Dubhgall's head, and Dubhgall slid to his knees. Lachlan turned in confusion to face Calach, whose presence there was completely unexpected. The branch crashed with a thud against Lachlan's cheek, and Lachlan reeled wildly into a tree.

Calach turned toward Berchan.

Berchan, bewildered by Calach's speed and agility, spun around to face him.

Calach stooped and grasped a smooth, oval rock. As he straightened, he threw the rock with precision, and it cracked loudly against Dubhgall's head. Dubhgall crumpled to the ground beside Berchan, grasping his bleeding head.

Berchan lunged toward Calach, who seemed to vanish from the spot where he had stood. Berchan grasped at the air as he lost his balance and skidded on the sod. He whirled on his knees toward a cry of pain from behind him, in time to see Calach wrenching Lachlan's arm, twisting it at an impossible angle behind him.

Berchan lunged toward Calach. He threw his full weight against Calach and wrapped his arms tightly around him. Berchan's momentum pulled Calach away from Lachlan, and a hollow crack resounded as Lachlan's shoulder came free of its socket.

Dubhgall had recovered, and he threw himself headlong into Calach's gut, knocking the wind from Calach's lungs. Berchan threw Calach gasping to the ground.

As Calach struggled to his knees, Dubhgall gripped his elbows from behind and pulled them backwards until they pressed painfully together. Dubhgall swung Calach in an arc until he faced the seething Berchan. Berchan advanced with an evil sneer.

Berchan swung hard, bringing the back of his hand across Calach's face. Calach flushed red as blood trickled from the corner of his mouth. Berchan cocked his arm for a second, massive blow.

A loud *thunk* rang out, and a groan escaped from Dubhgall's throat as he loosened his grip on Calach. Everyone looked in shock to see Maerla standing defiantly by the tall, thick oak. She held a second rock in her hand, half-cocked in case she was forced to let it fly.

Calach took immediate advantage of Maerla's timely distraction. He slipped his right arm free of Dubhgall's loosened grip as Lachlan approached once again from the side, and he landed a blow squarely across Lachlan's jaw.

Calach wrenched himself free of his bewildered captors and circled around Berchan, so that he was facing all four of his foes. Suemas remained helplessly rooted to the ground.

Berchan lunged again, swinging his dagger widely as he bore down upon Calach. Calach attempted to dodge Berchan's grasp, but Berchan's dagger caught his shoulder, its dull blade tearing a deep gash in the muscle. Calach winced in pain, and wrapped his fingers tightly around his own dagger, tucked into his leather belt.

As Berchan prepared to rush again, Calach was distracted by the sight of Dubhgall loping awkwardly toward Maerla, his face twisted in rage. Berchan's shoulder slammed heavily into Calach's left side, below his bleeding shoulder. Pain seared his side as Calach heard several of his ribs crack, and the momentum spun him hard into a thick tree trunk. His face cracked solidly into the rough and widely grooved bark. Bright lights flickered at the edges of his vision, and the taste of blood filled his mouth. The inside of his cheek had split deeply against his teeth. His vision blurred, and he began to feel numb.

Calach fumbled again for his own dagger, retrieving it with difficulty from his belt. He turned to meet Berchan's next lunge. Berchan's filthy blade glinted dully in his clenched right hand.

"Don't do this!" Calach screamed, as he dodged again. Berchan growled as he grasped at his nimble target. "Don't do this!" Calach cried again.

Berchan stopped to glower at Calach. His mouth twisted into a menacing sneer.

"Why would I not? You're suddenly afraid to fight?"

Calach glanced toward Maerla. Dubhgall was shaking her violently, her hand clenched in his, as he struggled to rip the rock from her grasp.

"You don't want to do this!" Calach screamed. "This is foolishness! This is wrong!"

Berchan lunged again, screaming "I'll kill you, you stupid dog!"

Calach steeled himself against the force of Berchan's next impact. Berchan slammed solidly into Calach's unyielding body. Every muscle in Calach's body held rigid, but he shuddered under the blow.

Berchan's eyes grew wide in dismay as he realized that Calach's dagger had pierced his side. Looking down, he saw Calach's fist pressed against him, holding the dagger's gleaming handle. He knew that the blade was buried inside him.

Berchan tried to cry out, but could not. He only gurgled as his limbs began to convulse, and tremors shuddered through his chest. He slowly sagged, growing limp, and his body slid weakly to the ground. Calach's dagger slid free as he fell.

Calach stood motionless, his face frozen in shock. He held the bloody dagger in his hand as he looked down at the dying boy. His thoughts returned to Maerla.

Calach turned toward Maerla in time to see Dubhgall bringing the rock that he had torn from her hand down firmly against the side of her head. Maerla's head snapped sharply to the right, and she was unconscious.

Dubhgall sat motionless atop Maerla's twitching body. His hand trembled as he clutched the rock, now stained with Maerla's blood.

Calach was certain that the blow had killed Maerla. He screamed and charged Dubhgall. He was suddenly stopped in his path and brought to the ground, his legs restrained by Lachlan's arms gripped tightly around his legs. As Calach fell prone to the ground, he twisted his neck around in time to see Dubhgall coming at him with the same rock with which he had felled Maerla. Calach struggled wildly, but only for a moment before searing pain overwhelmed his senses.

After the first blow, numbness quickly set in. Calach was vaguely aware of several more blows to his face, and many to his back and his legs. The blows seemed to be moving farther away, until they seemed barely to touch him at all.

Someone, Dubhgall, he thought, was screaming something into his face. He couldn't make out the words, and he thought for a moment that they were screaming at him in some foreign tongue. Only one word seemed to keep coming through to him, loud and angry and clear.

"Murderer! Murderer!"

What do they mean? he wondered. *Are they murdering me? Did I murder...?* Calach's stomach churned at the distant and murky realization that he had probably killed Berchan. He was the murderer, they were saying. And now they were murdering him. His churning stomach began to empty, and Calach's consciousness slipped quickly away.

5

Judgment

THE BOYS MOVED AS QUICKLY as they could through the trees toward the village. The weight of Berchan's body slowed them as they dragged it on a litter they had hastily fashioned out of branches and boughs. The litter caught on the brush as they passed, and Suemas limped painfully, trying desperately to keep up.

One side of the litter slid suddenly into a gully, and Berchan's body rolled awkwardly to the ground toward Suemas. Suemas leapt sideways into a thistle patch. He let out a blood-curdling scream as thistle thorns stabbed his badly injured foot.

"So pleasing to look at, yet so painful to tread upon," Lachlan observed, smirking at the thistles. Suemas glared angrily. Lachlan and Dubhgall heaved as they rolled Berchan's body back onto the litter, and they continued on.

The boys devised an account of the incident that they would present upon their return to the village. They argued and debated the details, but eventually they agreed unanimously on an account that would bear the scrutiny that they knew would be intense. Berchan, Calach, and

Maerla were dead; the shock of this affair would reverberate deeply through the Caledonii tribe, for a very long time to come. Their explanation would not be lightly received.

Dusk had fallen when the battered, exhausted boys dragged Berchan's lifeless body out of the woods that fringed Muthill. A gasping crowd gathered to witness their procession toward the village square.

Frangag's eyes narrowed when she recognized the hooligans who had tormented her so, and she wondered what trouble they had brought to the tribe on this day. She looked around instinctively for Calach, her intuition nagging persistently at her gut. Anxiety arose within her as she noted his absence.

The elders gathered in front of the meeting hall to hear the boys' account.

"He was a lunatic!" Lachlan gasped in horror. "Like a wild animal, he was! Just look at what he has done…" Lachlan pointed at Berchan, lying upon the litter.

"Who?" Fionnlagh, the senior elder, demanded. "Who did this?"

There were gasps and cries from the crowd as everyone pushed closer for a look at the dead boy and his battered friends. Gabhran made his way close to the center of the crowd.

"It was Calach," Dubhgall declared. Gabhran's eyes widened in shock. His heart pounded as he stared at his brother's accuser.

This cannot be true, Gabhran thought to himself. By the gods, do not let this be true!

Fionnlagh and the other elders looked at one another in dismay.

"Calach?" Aodhan asked in disbelief. Aodhan was second elder to Fionnlagh, and one of Tearlach's closest friends. Aodhan had watched Calach grow since birth, and he had never seen any hint that the boy was capable of this misdeed. "I cannot believe that Calach could have done this."

"Explain, slowly and carefully, how this happened," Fionnlagh commanded.

Lachlan was the appointed spokesman among the accomplices.

"We were walking through the woods," Lachlan began. He appeared to be catching his breath, and he rubbed his throbbing shoulder as he spoke. "We heard loud voices coming from far away, and then a girl screamed."

Dubhgall continued. "We ran as fast as we could to see what was amiss."

"We reached a ridge," Lachlan added. "We looked down to see a scuffle. That Calach was pushing the girl down. He forced her to the ground, and she screamed again."

"Berchan said that we should help her," Suemas said, nodding in the direction of his dead friend, "to get her away from Calach before he hurt her."

"We followed Berchan," Lachlan said. "We had no choice. We couldn't leave the girl to that wolf." Lachlan held his head high, proud of his contribution to their noble deed. His face then turned solemn. "He turned on us like a lunatic. He was painted up all warrior-like, and there was fierce madness in his eyes.

"We went for the girl, to pull her away from Calach. Berchan went straight for Calach. They fought for a moment, and then Calach pulled his dagger. Berchan barely had time to draw his own before Calach stabbed him in the side.

"We went after him, but we weren't fast enough on our feet. He pulled his dagger from Berchan's side and turned against us. We rushed him all together, to overcome him." Lachlan paused, and he turned to the other boys. Someone should continue the story, so it wouldn't seem as though Lachlan were making it up.

"I knocked the dagger away," Dubhgall said. "He picked up a rock to hit me with, but I pushed him away, and he slid on the moss. I think that made him even madder than he already was. He got to his feet and rushed me, swinging that rock. I dodged and tried to trip him, or grab him, but he slipped my grasp.

"He swung wildly and hit the girl with the rock," Lachlan said. "The force of it cracked her skull."

A collective gasp escaped from the crowd as Lachlan looked around to gauge their belief. Dubhgall and Suemas looked to the elders.

"That's when I killed him," Lachlan said, turning to look squarely at the elders. Gabhran's mouth opened in mute horror. Tearlach sank to his knees. "Or at least I think I did. I'm pretty sure he was dead when we left him."

"And the girl?" Fionnlagh asked quietly.

"The girl?" Lachlan repeated. "She was dead."

"Yes," Fionnlagh said thoughtfully, "so you said." He looked around, searching for something unseen. "Where," he continued, "is her body?"

Lachlan stared stupidly back at Fionnlagh, mute.

"It's back in the woods," Suemas clumsily offered.

"The three of you carried your friend all this way," Fionnlagh sighed. "Was it so much more important that you bring his dead body here, and not the girl? Is he so much lighter than she, that you could not bear the girl, if only for the sake of her family?"

Lachlan stood speechless, confused. They had not thought of that aspect of their scheme. He cursed himself for not thinking of it, and Fionnlagh noted his inward reproach. Fionnlagh's steady, piercing gaze held fast upon Lachlan.

"And you there," Aodhan the elder called out. He pointed toward Suemas, who leaned awkwardly against Dubhgall, trying to keep his weight off of his injured foot. "What happened to you?"

Lachlan flinched.

"He shot an arrow through my foot!" Suemas said.

"*Who* shot an arrow through your foot?" Aodhan asked.

"Calach!" Suemas said, as though the question were foolish. He smirked stupidly at Lachlan, whose jaw was suddenly tense.

The elders looked at one another quietly, carefully masking their thoughts. Aodhan turned back towards Suemas, with a steady, solemn gaze.

"Calach shot you," Aodhan began, slowly and with purpose, "with an arrow...through the foot...at close range...while struggling with the girl, in the midst of your charge."

Suemas's expression changed from indignation to befuddlement. He looked down at his foot, confused.

"At what point in the scuffle," Aodhan continued, staring hard at Lachlan, "which you so precisely described, was Calach able to string his bow? To fire a clean shot through the foot of a boy who was coming up hard upon him, in numbers?"

The boys were at a loss to answer. After a silence, the elders instructed the boys to remain where they stood, and to wait. Melcon, the Caledonii king, accompanied the elders as they entered the meeting hall, closing the door behind them. The conspirators stood nervously shuffling their feet, and shooting admonishing looks at one another.

The large, sturdy meeting hall had stood for hundreds of years, at the center of ancient Muthill, and had been the site of countless trials, commendations, debates, and calls to war.

Only the most venerated of elders held the honor of sitting in one of the seven heavy oak chairs at the front of the hall. The center chair was the largest, and it was reserved for the chief elder, or on the rare occasion when the matter at hand was sufficiently weighty, for the king.

Melcon took the center chair. A hearing would be held here today, the shock of which would reverberate through Muthill for a very long time. The events of the day would be branded forever into the fabric of this ancient tribe.

Awareness crept slowly into Calach's shrouded mind. His first awareness was that he was paralyzed, or weighted down by something enormously heavy. He could not open his eyes to look around him, to see what was holding him down.

He realized that heavy rain was drenching him, stinging the swollen skin on his face, and rolling in rivulets down his cheeks to the back of his neck. A tiny tributary found its way into his nostril, and he choked violently when it flooded into his throat. Involuntary coughing sent spears of burning agony radiating from his ribs throughout his body. The aching pressure in his head made it feel like it would explode.

Calach's eyes had been cemented shut by the blood that caked their lids. He tried desperately to open them, rubbing awkwardly at his crusty mask. His memory of what had just transpired began to fade back into focus, but the incident seemed to have occurred ages ago. He wondered how long he had been laying in this condition.

He suddenly remembered Maerla. His body tensed as he tried to spring up, but failed. His head fell back against the ground with a shattering thud. He ignored it and summoned the strength to try again.

Calach crawled painfully, for what seemed hours, until he reached Maerla's motionless body. He held his cheek close to her face. Relief overcame him when he felt the faint wisp of her breath against his cheek. He pulled off his sash and held its drenched cloth to her forehead. He whispered into her ear, and he willed her to hear him, and to awaken.

Several minutes passed before Maerla's eyes began to flutter. Another passed before she turned her pain-filled eyes toward Calach. She forced a weak smile at the sight of him.

"You're alive," she croaked. She closed her eyes in relief.

"And you," Calach said. "By the gods. I saw the blow. I was sure you were gone."

Calach and Maerla pulled one another up and onto their feet. Every step was torment as they made their way toward their village, which seemed to be thousands of miles away. They pressed on, determined to reach home. Calach promised Maerla that he would die if he must to get her home. She half-joked that he should not be so willing to make such a vow, being so close to fulfilling it.

After several hours that seemed like days, they came upon Maerla's home. Calach's weak knock upon the door was immediately answered by a powerful man with tearful, red-rimmed eyes. The sight of them shocked Maerla's father, Niall, beyond words. As Maerla's mother approached from behind, he let out a wordless yell.

"They said you killed our daughter," Maerla's father said.

"You're alive!" Liusaidh sobbed in relief. She rushed to throw her arms around her shivering, disheveled daughter.

"What happened," Niall demanded of Calach.

"Calach saved my life," Maerla declared. "Berchan and the others were hurting me. Calach risked his life to save mine."

"Then come with me," Niall commanded, through tightened lips. Calach winced in pain as Niall grasped him by his wounded shoulder and hurried him toward the meeting hall. Liusaidh and Maerla rushed to follow them, struggling to match their pace.

The elders had convened a hearing. The boys had been called inside, along with their families. Spectators crowded in until there was room for no more. The room buzzed with nervous energy and premature speculation. Fionnlagh, the senior elder, made his third call for order, and it finally silenced the crowd to a low murmur.

Fionnlagh ordered Lachlan to recount the tale, warning him not to leave out even the slightest of details, even if he thought them insignificant. Lachlan cleared his throat and began, glancing a warning to his accomplices to stick with the story.

"We were walking through the woods–"

"*Who*, exactly, was with you?" Aodhan demanded. Lachlan shot an involuntary look of annoyance toward Aodhan, who crossed his arms and slowly leaned back.

"Berchan," Lachlan answered, "Suemas, and Dubhgall."

"Continue," Fionnlagh commanded.

"We heard screaming. It was a girl, screaming. We went to see what was amiss."

"Just screaming?" Cailean, another of the elders asked softly.

"And yelling. We heard Calach yelling."

"Did you know it was Calach?" asked Aodhan.

"Yes. Well…no, not at first. Not until we got to the top of the crest. Then we saw him pushing himself onto the girl."

"What girl?" Diarmaid, another elder, asked.

"It was Maerla," Lachlan answered. The elders looked at one another in silence. They bid the boy to go on. They listened closely, stopping him from time to time to clarify something, or to make him retell some part of the story.

Lachlan was still uncertain about how to explain the part about the arrow, and so he deftly avoided it in his retelling. Aodhan would not let it slip.

"You need to back up and repeat something," Aodhan said, holding up his hand, "because something still doesn't make sense to me." He was deeply perplexed, and he stared hard into Suemas's eyes as he continued. "Tell me again how Calach managed, with four strapping lads bearing down upon him, and a struggling girl in his arms, to string up an arrow and let it fly, in close quarters, with such precision that poor Suemas will be limping for the rest of his life."

A commotion outside the hall drew all eyes toward the heavy double doors, and Lachlan exhaled softly, thankful for a timely reprieve. The spectators watched in silence as Maerla's father, Niall, pulled the doors wide and stormed into the room. Niall beckoned to Fionnlagh, who sent Diarmaid to speak with him outside.

Lachlan suspected that Niall was calling for Calach's death, if he were still alive, and the banishment of Calach's family from the tribe. Lachlan grinned smugly to himself

As the crowd resettled, Aodhan returned an expectant gaze toward Lachlan. He motioned for Lachlan to give his answer.

"The arrow?" Aodhan prodded.

"I don't remember," Lachlan clumsily answered. "So much was happening. I don't know how or when he did that. I know it happened, but I can't describe it."

"No, I thought not," Aodhan replied. "Conveniently, every detail seems clear except for that one." He shook his head in disbelief.

Diarmaid returned to the hall. Before he resumed his seat, he leaned and whispered to Fionnlagh for a moment. Fionnlagh nodded, and Diarmaid sat.

"So, in summary," Fionnlagh said abruptly, "the four of you rushed to defend a defenseless girl from the violence of that half-crazed Calach. Calach turned to fight, and he drew his dagger, killing Berchan…the strongest of you. Then, somewhere in the commotion, he strung an arrow and shot it through Suemas's foot.

"The two of you," Fionnlagh continued, indicating Lachlan and Dubhgall, "attempted to subdue this wild boy, who, having lost his dagger, picked up a rock and attacked you with it. He missed you both, and instead he struck the girl, killing her. Maerla is dead. Is my understanding correct so far?"

Lachlan nodded weakly at the summary, which suddenly somehow sounded ridiculous. He glanced at the others, who stood motionless, and he glared at them until they dutifully nodded in unison. Fionnlagh continued.

"That's when you, Lachlan, struck and killed Calach. You yourself did that."

Lachlan nodded again.

"If you had not attempted to rescue this girl, Calach would surely have done her great harm," Fionnlagh said.

"Yes," Lachlan agreed. Fionnlagh regarded Lachlan thoughtfully for a moment, and then continued.

"In spite of your heroic attempt, however, Calach succeeded in killing both Berchan and the girl, and shooting an arrow through Suemas's foot."

Lachlan nodded yet again, but with little enthusiasm.

"And Calach is dead," Fionnlagh declared. "So he has paid justly for his crime."

Lachlan nodded feebly.

"Justice has been done," Fionnlagh said, nodding his approval, "and the three of you have proven yourselves to be only marginally heroic in your failure to save Maerla's life. We should be lauding you for the courage of your attempt. We'll come to that, of course. But first we need to make clear just one troubling detail of this terrible incident."

Lachlan looked at Fionnlagh with a hint of trepidation as the doors to the meeting hall opened, and four silhouetted figures quietly entered the stifling room.

"How can you explain to us, Lachlan...," Fionnlagh asked, indicating the figures entering the hall, "*this?*"

Lachlan and his friends turned in horror to see Calach, drenched and badly beaten, and Maerla, her hair matted with thick, dried blood, accompanied by Niall and Liusaidh on either side, their arms firmly supporting Lachlan's brutalized victims.

The meeting hall was stunned into silence as the spectators looked in horror upon the three accomplices, who hung their heads in shame.

"Calach saved my life," Maerla said, her voice ringing out through the hall, shaking but resolute. "These boys laughed like jackals while their fiendish friend tried to defile me. Calach's arrow made the stupid one howl, distracting the others from their assault."

Murmuring filled the room, almost drowning Maerla's declaration. Fionnlagh stood and raised his hands for silence, which ensued. Maerla continued.

"Berchan threw himself upon Calach's dagger, which he held in self defense. This one," Maerla spat, pointing contemptuously at Dubhgall, "smashed a rock against my head and left me for dead. Then they all – and it took all of them to do it – beat Calach near to death. They left him there, as they did me, for dead." Maerla glared at the three boys with contempt. "You failed in even that, you wretched pigs!"

Maerla's words were followed by a cacophony of cries of condemnation, exclamations of dismay, and urgent calls for justice. Fionnlagh signaled once again for silence, and he requested that all but the elders leave the hall.

Men were appointed to escort the boys under guard to their confinement, to await the judgment of the elders. Aodhan requested that Niall and Maerla remain behind for a moment, and that Liusaidh and Calach stay close outside the doors.

Maerla turned to Calach with a weary smile. Her eyes showed gratitude and admiration, but also sadness for the brutality that he had suffered on her behalf. Calach returned a compassionate smile, and it clearly conveyed to her that he had not the slightest regret, for either his actions or their consequences.

"I can't bear to think of what would have happened had you not arrived," she said. "I thank you, with all my heart." She squeezed Calach's hand. "I will remember what you did for me, for all of my days."

Calach nodded slowly. He too was glad that he had been there in Maerla's moment of need. But he would also remember, and share with Maerla the scars of this day, until the end of his own. More than anything, he knew that despite any previous ambitions he might have hoped to pursue with Maerla, his association with her would forever be tainted by the trauma they had shared, and by the stench of Berchan's death at his hands.

Calach nodded gently, and said nothing as he turned to walk outside the meeting hall. Maerla instinctively understood the realizations with which he was struggling.

Calach waited outside in the misty rain, a short distance from where Liusaidh stood. He knew that she wanted to console him, and to shower him with gratitude for his bravery in saving her daughter, but he could not bear the weight of such attention. He had killed someone, and it was more than enough for him to labor under the weight of that truth. Calach deftly avoided Liusaidh's searching gaze.

At long last, the elders called Calach into the hall. He stood before them, straight and firm, but with his eyes cast downward in shameful respect.

"Calach," Aodhan said, "look at us, so that we may speak to you sincerely."

Calach complied, and his eyes met those of each elder, finally resting upon Melcon, who stared at him with intensity.

"Your actions in this matter," Fionnlagh began, "were brave. Some might say foolhardy, as well. But you did what a warrior would do: you subordinated your own well-being to the welfare of another. You came to the aid of the defenseless, at the likely expense of your life. You did precisely what any of the accomplished warriors who sit before you would have done."

"I have taken a life," Calach interjected. His sorrow was evident.

"A life was thrust upon you," Aodhan corrected.

"You did what had to be done," Fionnlagh continued. "You did nothing to cause its necessity. You did more than many others would have done in your place, and your courage exceeded that of the average man. We commend you today, young Calach, for your courage, your strength, and your honor. You have earned admiration for your name."

"The others...," Calach ventured.

"...are no longer your concern. Justice will be done here today," Fionnlagh answered.

Calach nodded his understanding.

"You're free to go," Aodhan said. "But allow me one final word of warning." Calach turned his attention to his father's friend. "Ensure that you never become too willing to use your weapons of war. While justified, any death is tragic, and any war a dreadful devastation upon all who take part. I think you have learned that today. Carry the lesson with you."

"I will," Calach assured him. He bowed deeply before the elders, who looked at one another, appreciative of his respect.

As Calach left the hall, Melcon rose from his chair, and he motioned for the elders Diarmaid and Aodhan to follow. Melcon also beckoned toward Tearlach, who had been standing in the shadows at a far side of the hall. Tearlach's movement was Calach's first awareness of his presence, and he looked to his father in surprise. Tearlach was beaming with proud satisfaction.

As they left the hall, Melcon sent Diarmaid to summon the families of the three delinquents to the hall for judgment.

"Walk with me," Melcon said to Tearlach, Calach, and Aodhan. The four of them walked in silence for a distance before Melcon finally spoke.

"The judgment of the elders was wise," Melcon finally said.

"It pained me to hear their accusations against my son," Tearlach said, "and their claim to have left him dead." To Calach, he said, "I knew that they were lying against you, my son."

Melcon waved the matter away. It was finished, and there was an issue at hand that was of greater import.

"You will soon enter your twelfth year, will you not?" Melcon asked Calach.

"In the spring of next year," Calach replied.

"Seven months," Melcon clarified. "You're anxious for your passage, are you not? Anxious to join your first hunt? Anxious for the rites?"

"I am," Calach nodded.

"We Cruithne wait, as a custom, until the end of the twelfth year before we expect a young man to demonstrate his fitness for manhood."

Melcon walked on thoughtfully, admiring the village, the oaks and the birch, and the industrious Caledonii as they went about their business around the village.

"It's a rare and remarkable occasion when such a thing occurs unexpectedly, before the end of the twelfth year," Melcon continued, "when some event demonstrates clearly that a young man has already made the passage."

Tearlach squeezed Calach's shoulder in anticipation. Calach winced in pain.

Melcon stopped in his tracks. He turned to face Calach, regarding his proud and resilient demeanor, yet evident in spite of his grueling experience. Melcon gazed long into Calach's steady eyes, and then he turned to Tearlach and spoke, while Aodhan witnessed the proclamation.

"Your son is a man. He is among the finest of men I have known. His strength and his courage bring honor to your name. I would be proud to call him my own, but none shall ever deny you that honor. His passage has been accomplished." With those words, Melcon had declared Calach's status as a warrior of the Caledonii tribe, and as a man.

Melcon looked kindly into Calach's face.

"Honor the Caledonii name. Live in the spirit of Cruithne. This day you have made me proud to call you a son of my tribe."

Melcon turned and began to walk back toward the meeting hall. Aodhan nodded and smiled at Calach and Tearlach, and then turned to follow the king. Tearlach threw his arm around Calach's aching shoulders, and they headed toward home for an evening that Calach would remember fondly for the rest of his days.

In the meeting hall, the distraught families of the three wayward boys and the dead Berchan sat huddled, waiting, wringing their hands and bemoaning the misfortune brought upon them by their sons. The elders sat quiet and stern. All arose upon Melcon's return to the hall.

Fionnlagh vacated the center seat, making way for his king, and Muir, the most junior elder, moved to stand behind the one he had relinquished to Fionnlagh. When all took their places, Melcon motioned for the elders to sit, while he alone remained standing in front of his chair.

Melcon remained expressionless as he declared the elders' judgment against the boys.

"This day has seen incalculable and grievous injustice, and in the face of it, unyielding character and strength. The seriousness of the transgressions of this unruly mob cannot, and will not go unpunished. I have heard the judgment of the elders, and I am in complete agreement. The penalty for the crimes of your sons will be executed without delay.

"Each of your families is banished, forever and without reprieve. The dishonor brought upon you by your sons is unforgivable, and has rendered you unworthy of association with this tribe. Your presence here will be tolerated not one more day; by this time tomorrow you will be gone from here forever. You are to leave far from Caledonii land, and never to return, except under penalty of death."

Melcon turned to Dubhgall, who had attempted to murder Maerla.

"Your offense is the most grievous of all. You attempted to murder a daughter of this tribe. You came here lying to us, in the belief that you had indeed committed her murder. My judgment is that you are, *in fact*, a murderer, since you were content to count yourself one."

Dubhgall's mother cried out as she realized the significance of Melcon's ruling. Melcon continued, ignoring her anguish.

"You will suffer the penalty for murder, without delay. Your family will witness your execution this night, and then they will leave here with nothing at the first light of day. All that they possessed will go to your intended victim. Justice has been done here today."

Dubhgall's family wailed upon hearing their son's fate, and at the forfeiture of all they possessed. All of those gathered lamented the hardship they would surely endure.

Banishment meant endless wandering in search of a tolerant tribe, which they were unlikely to find among the Picts. More likely, they would be forced to flee to the south, into the arms of the hostile and enslaved Pretani. Among the Pretani, their best hope would be for acceptance as servants, or workers in the fields, or soldiers of the lowest of ranks in the Pretani detachments of the Roman army. Whatever their fate, their life as they had known it had ended.

"Girom!" Calach cried from the clearing on his private ridge. The sky was as cold and dark as his miserable disposition. His heart-rending cry resounded across the valley, coming back to him in echoes through the mist. "I need you now," he said softly, almost whispering, in pain. Calach stood there in the silence and waited, straining his ears for a sound.

He felt a figure approaching from behind him. He turned to look, but he could only make out a faint and featureless form that seemed to glide rather than walk in his direction. As it came nearer it grew more defined, and he could finally make out the old, familiar face. Calach marveled at the impression that Girom has simply materialized, and had not approached from any particular direction.

"I'm here," Girom said softly. The gravelly gruffness of his voice was surprisingly capable of conveying a tenderness that Calach found protective and reassuring.

"I've killed someone," Calach said slowly, softly. "I've killed one of my own. I've taken the life of another."

Girom stood silent, observing Calach's turmoil with deep sadness. He moved to place a hand on Calach's shoulder.

"Yes, you have killed someone," Girom conceded. "I've the impression it was not your first choice." Calach shook his head slowly.

"Did you do so with rage in your heart?" Girom asked.

Calach nodded solemnly. "There was rage," he said mournfully.

Girom nodded, tightening his lips.

"Did you try to stop it from happening?"

Calach looked up, remembering.

"I begged him to stop."

"Did you kill because you had been wronged?" Girom asked.

Calach looked straight at Girom then, in surprise.

"No! I had not been wronged." Calach puzzled, as fragments of Girom's previous advices and admonitions returned to him.

"You killed, then, for no good reason? You killed someone who had done you no wrong?" Girom pressed.

"He wronged Maerla," Calach answered. "He was going to violate her."

Girom nodded again. He allowed Calach time to think on his words.

"You protected her, then," Girom finally offered.

"I did."

"Against what odds?"

"Four boys. Bullies, all of them. Well...," he paused, "three, actually." He grinned slightly. "One was...otherwise engaged." Girom raised questioning eyebrows. "I had shot an arrow through his foot. He couldn't move from where he stood."

Girom tried hard not to laugh, but in vain. Loud and heartfelt laughter escaped, ringing through the trees and echoing back. He quickly regained his composure.

"This is not a matter of mirth," he scolded, clearly rebuking himself. Then he turned solemn. "Did you enjoy taking his life?"

Girom gazed intently into Calach's troubled eyes. He already knew the answer to his question.

"No!" Calach exclaimed. "I felt justified, but I did not enjoy it. I felt forced to do it. I do regret that Maerla witnessed it. It has haunted me since the moment it happened."

"And what taste lingers from the spilling of this blood?" Girom prodded.

Calach looked firmly at Girom. His eyes hardened, and his lips curled into an ugly grimace.

"Bitterness. Foul bitterness. I want to empty my stomach until there is nothing left to spew. I do not want to carry this blood on my hands, and I do not want to carry this memory through my life."

"My dear Calach…," Girom began. He grasped Calach's shoulders firmly, turning the boy to face him. Calach winced as his injured shoulder throbbed. "…my dear and noble boy. Remember what I told you so long ago. It appears to me that you have not truly forgotten. But for this moment, let's bring it to mind. You were forced – against your will – to stand and fight for something you knew to be right. You fought against something shameful in the defense of nobler things. You sought not vengeance, but defense of the defenseless. You sought not to dominate, but to protect. You righted a wrong by the only means permitted you. It was not your choice, but Berchan's, that this should happen."

Calach was startled by Girom's mention of Berchan's name. Calach had not spoken it to him, and he wondered how much the old man really knew, and how he had come to know it.

"You knew, then?" Calach asked in wonder.

"The moment it happened," Girom replied, with a wry and mischievous smile.

Calach stood silent, perplexed. Girom continued.

"You were not given a choice. You did not take Berchan's life. Berchan forced his life upon you. He had no right to do so, but he did it, and you must bear it. He caused you pain with which you will struggle for the rest of your life. The bitterness will not leave your mouth, but will remain as a constant reminder, forever.

"Remember, too, that I told you that the day you take life with pleasure, the day you hunger for blood in revenge, then you will have surely lost much. That day has yet to come. You stand here before me having taken a life and lost nothing, but rather having gained the assurance that you are a just and noble soul. Mourn for the life that you have been forced to take, but know that you remain unbroken, and undefeated by the evil of men."

Girom stepped back slowly, almost drifting across the damp, moss-covered ground. His features grew dim, turning softer, and harder to ascertain. Calach stood speechless, filled with a mixture of wonder and calm reassurance. He knew that Girom was right, and he was now beginning to suspect the true nature of Girom's essence.

Calach watched as the shadows enveloped the fading figure. He felt as though Girom had somehow infused his soul with certainty and strength, calming the tumult of the trauma that had shrouded his heart.

Calach dearly wished that Girom would not leave.

6

Romans

THE LEGION MARCHED steadily northward along a rocky, overgrown trail. The sun rose inexorably higher, and grew increasingly hotter by the minute. Its glare blinded the soldiers as it reflected off of their heavily polished armor, and sweat streamed down their strained and reddened faces.

A transformation had taken place in the Pretani lands south of Calach's home. After centuries of isolation from the tumultuous history of the vast continent to the east of their small island, the Pretani had finally come to face its smoldering threat.

Romans were in control of the Pretani lands and tribes after years of brutal conquest and final capitulation. The Pretani had resisted, most vehemently with a massive and costly insurrection led by the enigmatic Queen Boudiccea. But the Romans ultimately prevailed, and the Pretani had since become essentially Roman.

After the Boudiccean uprising was finally crushed, the decimated Britannic legions spent half a decade in recovery and another in resentful, if idle, occupation of lower Britannia. The moral blow

Boudiccea had inflicted upon the Romans would take years to fade
away. Its repercussions in Rome had brought chaos and devastation to
much of the Roman military's upper echelon.

The Britannic legions had replenished their ranks with new recruits
from Rome, and with conscripts from Britannia and from across the
conquered frontier, including many distant barbarian lands. The ranks
of the Roman army included eager citizen sons anxious to expand the
empire's realm, and slave-warriors captured in frontier conquests.

The ferocity of the Boudiccean uprising had engendered a vengeful
bloodlust among many of the Roman veterans of that conflict, most of
whom had been forced to remain in damnable Britannia. Even
barbarian soldier-slaves who had originally empathized with the Pretani
now thirsted for vengeance for the brutalities they endured in the
uprising. The losses inflicted upon them by the Pretani had been
immense, and the reward for their final victory was continued exile in
this distant, gloomy land.

Revolving provincial leadership that seemed most intent on
endearing and assimilating – Romanizing – the insolent Britannic
barbarians, strictly, and sometimes brutally, contained the soldiers'
smoldering resentments.

As the focus of the Governor of Britannia shifted wholly to the
assimilation process, and away from his restless ranks, discipline and
loyalty deteriorated and the soldiers grew unruly. Hostility brewed
between the Roman citizens and the slave-soldiers, especially those who
had survived the merciless decimation of the Germanic tribes.

The Roman army typically offered conquered captive warriors
several options, and for most the choice was clear. The proudest chose a
swift, defiant death, or a short and gory stint in the gladiators' ring. The
weakest faced a life of endless degradation in domestic service to
spoiled Roman citizens. Most chose to live out their lives in lengthy
service as infantry soldier-slaves, with the distant promise of hard-

earned Roman citizenship. Soldier-slaves made up almost half of the Roman army.

This restless amalgamation of Roman soldiers in Britannia longed for war. Any war anywhere would be better than the squalor into which they had become mired in this bitter land.

It was this condition to which Gnaeus Julius Agricola returned when he came to take command of the Twentieth Legion, and the governorship of Britannia. Agricola had proven his military prowess on the battlefields of Britannia years before. He had led a legion against the Boudiccean rebellion, under the apprenticeship of his mentor, Suetonius Paulinus.

Agricola's earlier time in Britannia had inspired his dreams to return one day as its governor, and to seize for himself the honor of finally and totally subduing these western islands in the name of the Emperor, and for the glory of Rome.

The Emperor badly needed the victory that Agricola sought. Embarrassing criticism had continued to mount as influential Romans grew increasingly weary of the continued failure of the protracted, and seemingly stalled, Britannic campaign. Agricola was eager to give the Emperor his critical victory, and to earn for himself the greatest honors of Rome.

"Welcome to Britannia, Governor, my dear old friend!" Quintus shouted, as Agricola and his escort approached the imposing Roman fort. "And to your new headquarters! Viroconium is now the most heavily defended fort in Britannia, and I am honored to call it your new home!"

Agricola dismounted with a pleasant smile. He stood holding his horse's reins and admiring the sturdy fortress that was home to the Twentieth Legion. A squire approached quickly and took the horse's reins. Agricola strode toward Quintus, and the two men embraced heartily. They kissed one another's cheeks, and then turned arm in arm to walk toward the fort's opened gates.

"I have been too long away," Agricola said. "I've grown soft in the luxury of Rome."

"I'd say not," Quintus argued. "You appear to maintain a gladiator's strength, and the keen eye of a well-practiced general. And now the bearing of a Governor."

Agricola feigned humble acceptance of Quintus's flattery.

"How goes it here, then, Quintus?" Agricola asked. "How are the men?"

"They will welcome you warmly," Quintus assured him. Quintus motioned to Aquila, the Ninth Legion Prefect, to organize Agricola's reception.

"I shall be anxious for that," Agricola nodded. "But tell me, please – what is the condition of the legions? What is their demeanor?"

"You have indeed been away too long," Quintus said solemnly. "The months have seemed to drag by us as years, with little to challenge or to amuse the anxious troops. Many long to return home. All long for action, or distraction of any kind."

The decayed condition of the Britannic Legions was to be the first of Agricola's challenges.

Quintus continued. "Word has preceded you that you have come to make ready for a major push into the north. Rumors of campaigns into the north have generated eagerness among the ranks. The men are waking from their stupor, and they are ready to follow your lead."

Agricola's arrival had indeed appeared to have sparked a spontaneous and self-directed reemergence of military discipline. Agricola's diary would reflect that he had arrived to find the troops mostly disciplined, ambitious, and well trained despite the profoundly failed leadership that he had come to rectify.

"Yes, indeed," Agricola said. "Vespasian is most anxious for a successful and resounding close to the Britannic campaign. He intends to announce for once and all that this land has been brought entirely under Roman dominion. There is little time to squander in that pursuit."

"The men will be glad to hear this," Quintus said, nodding excitedly.

At his reception, attended by the centurions of both the Ninth and the Twentieth Legions, Agricola spoke at length about the necessity of a forceful and relentless campaign into the north of Britannia. His pronouncements were met with general acclaim, and tremendous applause. The centurions responded most enthusiastically when Agricola made it clear that he, and the Emperor, would accept nothing less than total conquest and subjugation of the unruly northern tribes.

But first, Agricola warned, Roman control of the south must be solidified beyond question or dispute. Wales, to the west, and the Irish island beyond Wales, were to be utterly vanquished and subjected to Roman governance. Their lands would be fortified, and the legions would be fattened and trained, and infused by the knowledge and expertise of local conscripts.

All of this careful preparation, Agricola vowed, would build toward an inexorable, invincible march that would forever vanquish those peculiar and secretive barbarians to the north, long dreaded and generally avoided by the southern Britannic tribes.

Agricola intended to dissipate his conscripts' lingering fear of the northern Picts, by seizing decisive control of southern Britannia, and by swelling his own ranks to unprecedented and imposing levels. By the time they marched north, Agricola intended that there would be no hesitation among his legions to launch his massive campaign against the mysterious Picts.

The subjugation of the southern Britannia was total and complete, and preparations finally began for the long-awaited march against the Picts. Months of preparation, and the assessments of countless scouting parties returning from the north had bolstered Agricola's hopes for his success. He anticipated little organized resistance from the northern tribes.

The tribes appeared to be autonomous, the scouts assured him, and not united in any perceivable way. Agricola estimated the tribal population to be a little over eighty thousand, of whom less than thirty thousand were likely to be warriors of any account. He was confident that those warriors would never unite into a single, cohesive army. Even if they could, they would still be no match for the twenty four thousand experienced and well-trained legionnaires that would march against them.

Agricola would march forth with two Legions, each with more than eight thousand men and another four thousand in reserve. Some of his best soldiers had been borrowed from other, distant legions.

His own Twentieth Legion took the western flank. They would march northward a moderate distance inland from the western shore. The Ninth Legion, led by Quintus Petillius, took the eastern flank. Agricola's plan was to sweep to the northern coast, to establish Roman domination firmly and finally, through conquest or capitulation, over the entire population, and to end the Emperor's relentless frustration over Britannia.

The march began in early summer. Anxious and optimistic soldiers threw their heavy burdens high upon their shoulders and stepped eagerly into formation for the march. They shrugged off the minor discomforts of the seething sun as it beat upon their helmets, and the soggy bog land that seemed to suck their feet deeper with every step.

Tight formations threatened to unravel as soldiers vainly sought firmer ground upon which to march, but even that minor frustration didn't daunt their buoyant spirits. They were off to conquer the Picts! At last, the time had come. Nothing would stop them now.

The Ninth Legion was the first to encounter the Picts.

A short distance north of the River Tweed, the centurion Marcus led a troop of twenty scouts from the Ninth as it rode a short distance ahead of the legion. At the approach to a bend in the road, Marcus caught a brief movement in the brush several yards ahead, and just off the road. Squinting into the shadows, he counted a band of six tribal hunters hidden among the trees.

The hunters' skin had a ghostly bluish tint, as if it had been dyed, and their bodies were covered with strange and deeply etched markings, which he knew to be customary among the reclusive northern tribes. The tattoos were haunting pictures of grotesque demons and oddly proportioned animals. One of the hunters had a terrifying demonic face glaring from the ripples of his chest. Its eyes were red and menacing, and sharp fangs accented its bloody grimace. The dark blue tint of the skin on the hunters' faces contrasted starkly against the whites of their wild eyes. The chilling effect exaggerated their threatening gaze. The scouts wondered if these men weren't demons themselves, or at the very least, demon-possessed. The hunters were of the Pictish Selgovae tribe.

As the soldiers advanced along the rough, rocky road, which was more of a narrow path, the hunters stood motionless, watching warily from the edge of the woods. The hunters took note of the Romans' heavy armament and vast numbers, and they silently vanished into the woods. Marcus, the leader of the scout party, motioned for silence. The soldiers listened intently, but in vain, to identify the direction of the hunters' flight. Marcus shrugged. It was as if they had simply disappeared. The troop continued forward.

The scouts advanced several hundred yards before stopping abruptly in their tracks. Ahead of them, a larger group of Picts, numbering perhaps thirty, blocked the road. One of the Picts held up his hand and greeted the Romans in a strange tongue. The language resembled that of the Britannic tribes in the conquered south, but it was unintelligible to these Roman soldiers.

The soldiers stared silently at the Picts. It was obvious that they intended to resist the soldiers' advance. The leader of the Picts advanced toward to Romans, and Marcus signaled the others to prepare for a fight. The Pict raised his arms and spoke again in his tongue.

Marcus didn't waste a moment. He quickly dismounted and strode toward the Pict, with his left hand extended and his right held tensely at his side. In a flash Marcus drew his dagger, and before the Pict could react, it was buried to its hilt in his chest.

The Pict staggered backwards under the blow, but then quickly regained his balance. He rose to his full height and stood squarely in front of the stunned Roman, blood trickling down his chest from the buried blade. The Pict drew back his hand and struck Marcus full across the face, snapping his head backward and spinning him full around. Marcus now stood facing his soldiers, more stunned than he was before, and shaking off the blow. The Pict stood silently behind him, apparently in defiance of his own mortal wound.

Marcus placed his right hand on his sword. With a bellow, he drew it as he turned. He slashed viciously upward and through the center of the Pict's angry face.

The Pict fell heavily upon the ground. He pushed himself to his knees, and Marcus could not believe that he was still alive. The Pict glared at Marcus, his eyes still flashing amid the gore of his shattered face. He appeared ready to pounce, and Marcus thought he must surely be some inhuman beast. But the Pict slowly slumped, giving in to the massive loss of blood. He died quietly, never shifting his glare from Marcus's eyes, even as his own glazed over in death.

For a moment that seemed frozen in time, the rest of the Picts stood stunned, staring blankly at the unbelievable scene. The Romans shifted uneasily, and waited for the Pictish response. They soon had it.

As their shock dimmed, the Picts flew into a frenzied rage. With an unearthly chorus of bellows, they fell upon the Romans with vengeance.

In a matter of minutes, the entire Roman scout troop lay dead in the road. They barely had time to raise their weapons. Not another Pict was harmed.

As quickly as the fury had erupted, it was over, and the Picts were gone. They had vanished once again into the woods, melting into the shadows, and taking their dead leader with them. They left behind only the carnage drenched in Roman blood.

Not long after the Roman scouts were massacred on the desolate road, the bulk of the Ninth Legion came upon the grisly scene. Quintus, the Legate of the Ninth, who was riding at the head of the column, was among the first to perceive it. The column approached silently, and slowed as the scene sunk in. Quintus dismounted and strode to the mangled corpses of his scouts. He stared upon them for a long moment, and then he turned solemnly toward his centurions.

"Find them!" he bellowed. "Find the barbarians who did this and slaughter them, to the last! I want them dead, every last one!" Quintus turned, raging, "Lucius, take your men into the woods. You will track and kill these swine."

Lucius acknowledged the order with a tight nod.

"We will make camp two hours to the north," Quintus continued. "Meet up with us there when you have succeeded." Lucius came to attention, saluted, and turned to carry out his orders. He mustered his century of eighty skilled soldiers, and led them off the road and into the woods.

The legion marched on. At the appointed time they stopped to set up camp. As was the Roman custom, the soldiers set immediately to the fortifications. At the end of each day's march, fortifications were built, guards were drilled and placed, and the centurions met to plan the next day's march. By nightfall, all were hungry for sleep.

This night, though, sleep would evade these Romans. As the hours dragged on through the evening, they watched with anticipation for Lucius's return. Darkness fell, and still there was no sign. Long into the night the centurions sat with Quintus, and debated sending more soldiers back to search for the missing troop. They decided against it and waited through the night.

When morning broke, Lucius had still not returned, and trepidation overtook the camp. Quintus hid his growing alarm. He knew there was only one explanation for the troop's failure to return, and he knew that if there had been survivors, they would have made it to the fort by now. He decided against going back, and against sending another troop in search of the lost century. Instead, he sent messengers to the Twentieth Legion to the west, to advise Agricola of the loss.

Quintus began to suspect that the Romans may have underestimated these northern barbarians. He had still not seen even one of them. He had not so much as engaged in a minor skirmish. Yet he had already suffered the significant loss of over a hundred of his finest men.

"Muster the troops," Quintus barked at the centurions. "We'll push on. Double the scouts and close the ranks. Varius, you lead the scouts. Be alert! There will be no repeat of yesterday's disaster!"

The Romans broke camp and moved on. Varius, one of the legion's finest centurions, commanded one of the centuries of the first cohort. He was a seasoned veteran of the Germanic campaigns, a skilled soldier, and an excellent scout. He jumped at this chance to gain Quintus's favor. He selected the finest scouts from his century and set out ahead of the Legion.

A few hours into the morning march, as the sun was nearing its peak, the new scout unit began to see signs of a nearby town. There were fresh hoof marks in the road, and a number of paths worn into the brush along its edges. They halted at the sight of fresh horse dung on the road. Varius sent eight of the scouts back to alert Quintus. He sent eight more ahead to identify the location of the town. He warned them to use the utmost stealth, and to avoid detection at all costs. The town must not be alerted to their presence. Varius wondered to himself if his precautions were in vain. He suspected that their presence could already have been well noted.

Quintus and the rest of the first cohort centurions hurried forward to Varius's position when they received the news. Quintus was encouraged. After the developments of the last twenty-four hours, he knew that his soldiers were anxious for a real fight. They were disoriented by significant casualties in the absence of a real, planned battle. A good fight would help them to regain their footing. They waited anxiously for the advance scouts to return, and Quintus involuntarily held his breath. He realized that even against his steely resolve he had become unnerved. He exhaled deeply when he finally spied the approach of the returning scouts.

The scouts reported to Varius that the village was about a half mile ahead, and that its inhabitants appeared to be unaware of them, and unprepared for battle. There were close to a thousand villagers, each of them busy with their daily routine. About a third of them were adult men, able-bodied but unarmed. The village was an easy target, and ripe for attack. The town was Balloch, a village of the Selgovae tribe.

Quintus ordered two cohorts to the left, and two to the right, to flank the village and close in against any who tried to escape. The remaining six cohorts would hit the village head on. Quintus intended to focus the pent up rage of this legion on that town, and to exact vengeance for his massacred men. The legion began its maneuvers.

Quintus and the centurions were unaware of the glowering eyes that watched them from the depths of the woods.

Sioltach was Pretani, now of the Picts. He had been pressed into service of the Roman army when his tribe was overcome. He had rebelled with the Boudicceans and narrowly escaped with his life. A fugitive in his own land, he had found refuge among the Selgovae, who had welcomed him as a brother in arms.

Sioltach was proud to be called Selgovae, and he was happy in his new life, with a Selgovae wife, and with two strong sons of whom he was very proud.

Sioltach and thirty other tattooed hunters watched in silent horror from atop their horses among the trees that grew thick at the edge of the village. They knew that they alone could not stop this attack. Picts were scattered across the lowland valley, and into the highlands to the north, and they could never be assembled in time to defend the village of Balloch.

The best that the hunters could do was to ride through the village and raise the alarm, and to continue to the north to alert the other tribes to the Romans' presence. They wheeled their horses around and rode hard toward the unsuspecting village, letting out a war cry that rang through the trees.

Quintus cursed as the sound of the war cry reached his ears, and startled birds sprang from the surrounding trees. The Romans charged.

The villagers looked up in shock as the hunting party tore through the town, bellowing war cries and screaming at them to run into the woods and hide. Beyond the thundering hooves of the hunters' horses, they heard a more ominous sound. Just beyond their sight to the south, eight thousand pairs of armored feet pounded the earth in unison as the Romans advanced.

Orders were shouted and acknowledged, and the woods around the village seemed to come alive. Terror spread like wildfire through the town. Children screamed and ran as their mothers tried in vain to scoop them into their arms. Wide-eyed men embraced their wives in their wildly decorated arms, in a futile, frozen effort to shield them from harm. Dogs barked and roofs trembled, and the unison of a Roman battle mantra drowned the fading wild yells of the disappearing hunters. Those villagers that did not run stood fast, stolidly facing the advancing Roman ranks.

Sioltach wheeled his horse suddenly at the northern edge of town. He shouted at his fellow hunters to continue with the alarm while he stayed behind to attempt to save as many as he could. He desperately needed to find and rescue his family.

The Romans were close on his tail, entering the village from the south, and then from the east and west. The village was surrounded, and the only escape would be to the north.

Sioltach was frozen in his tracks at the sight of thousands of soldiers pouring through the trees and into the village. He backed his horse slowly into the cover of a thicket and dismounted, pulling the horse quickly to the ground.

Sioltach watched as the soldiers unleashed a fury that shocked even their general and the centurions into silence. The soldiers leveled years of pent up frustration and rage upon the helpless villagers. One soldier swung his sword ferociously upon a trembling man, his wife, and the baby they held between them until they lay in a bloody tangle against the house where they had huddled for protection. Babies were torn from their mothers' arms and viciously dismembered, while their watching mothers were raped by groups of soldiers, then killed. Villagers who hid inside houses were burned alive as the doors were blocked and the houses set afire.

Soldiers ravaged the dead bodies of teenage girls, and then severed and scattered their limbs. The atrocities these soldiers committed were unprecedented in General Quintus's vast knowledge of the often-brutal history of Roman conquest. Sioltach watched it all, his face a mask of frozen horror streaked with helpless tears.

In a little less than an hour, the carnage was almost complete. Throughout the town, bloodthirsty soldiers continued to violate the bloody corpses of slain wives and mothers. Dust began to settle on the blood-soaked ground, and the town slowly grew quiet. The soldiers had annihilated all but a small group of men, women, and children who were huddled in the midst of a ring of soldiers in the center of the town.

Sioltach caught sight of the terrified group of villagers who stood trembling as the soldiers closed in. His scream froze in his throat when he spied his wife among them.

Some of the encircled group begged in vain for mercy. Sioltach knew that their pleas would not be heard, since the soldiers had no grasp of their Pictish tongue.

Others stared angrily, in silence. All wore the same distinctive illustrations over the entirety of their exposed skin. Deeply etched drawings of eagles, wild boars, and other beasts mingled with interlocking circles, swirls, and zigzag lines. Sioltach marveled at the contrast between the captors and their captives – one group wild and free, at home in this secluded land, and the other polished and clean and out of place, as far from their home as they could be.

For a long moment, there was no movement. The surviving villagers endured an agonizing lull as the soldiers stared menacingly, sadistically drawing out this final, horrific moment. The villagers surveyed the mind-numbing scene just beyond the wall of soldiers, the scattered corpses of their families and the sea of blood soaking into the dusty ground, and many began to pray to their gods.

Finally, one hulking Roman turned slowly to another with a sickening, ghastly grin, and then he wheeled furiously with his sword, slicing down and into one of the villagers' heads. The man crumpled to the ground, and the rest of the soldiers sprang quickly into action.

Sioltach wailed as the soldiers methodically hacked off limbs or parts of limbs, killing the villagers slowly and one by one, as if savoring this last bit of carnage. Several soldiers turned to look idly in Sioltach's direction at the sound of his cry, but none made a move toward him.

Sioltach's wife stood straight and tall, resolute in the face of the soldiers' atrocity. She began to speak quickly to the soldiers as they engaged in their cruel game. Her voice was strong and clear, and her green eyes ablaze. In her Pictish language, she warned the soldiers of the swift and grave consequences of their brutality. Failing to understand her words, one Germanic soldier stood back from her in alarm. Sioltach thought he must have imagined her to be casting a pagan spell. With a ferocious swing of his sword, he severed her head mid-sentence.

The severed head tumbled to the ground, but it continued to stare at the German from where it fell, unnerving him further still. He backed away in fear, and then ran trembling as the other soldiers laughed after him.

Sioltach stood speechless, numbed and horrified. He let out another plaintive cry, and he stood to rush the evil men. His cry was cut short by a strong hand clasped across his face, and he was pulled roughly back into the cover of the brush. Sioltach's wild eyes darted from side to side, trying desperately to identify his captors.

Finally, the firm grip loosened, and Sioltach found himself in the arms of a fellow Selgovae hunter, just returned from the field to discover the unfolding carnage.

As the soldiers turned back to their slaughter, the woman's dead eyes were not the only ones that stared silently upon the blood-drenched scene. From the shadowy woods, the handful of hunters watched in anguished silence. There was nothing they could do. There was no one left to save, even if they could. They could only go north with the others to warn the rest of the tribes of the unexpected Roman incursion.

Sioltach slumped in abject realization that his family, his village, and everything that he had loved were now gone, taken by these rabid, ravenous thieves.

Quintus turned in slow circles in the center of the devastated village, absorbing the reality of what he had witnessed this past hour, and struggling with the stunned realization of the impact that years of languishing in Britannia had had on this legion.

He finally shook off the feeling and turned to the business at hand.

The soldiers completed the razing of the town, and set about building a solid garrison fort in its place. Quintus intended to leave fortifications along the route to provide defensible quarters throughout the region. On his triumphant return from final conquest of the north, he would garrison troops in these forts to solidify the Roman Empire's footing. He imagined the eventual gains he would make in expanding the Roman army by swelling his own ranks with what was left of the conquered barbarians. And Quintus had no doubt that these barbarians would be vanquished. He had no idea what rage his soldiers had just unleashed.

7

Wildfire

SIOLTACH AND THE BAND of Selgovae hunters rode furiously and non-stop for hours to reach the Caledonii lands, intent upon raising a suitable retaliation. They had witnessed the slaughter of most of their ancient tribe. Sioltach knew that Calach, the Caledonii warrior, now an accomplished military leader in his twenties, would be most willing to champion their cause.

Calach was thoughtful and idealistic. He was a natural leader among his people, and well respected by virtually all the Pictish tribes, having negotiated peaceful resolutions to some of the thorniest tribal disputes.

If the day should ever come when the diverse and independent tribes were to call one man King of all Picts, Calach would be a popular and viable candidate. Calach's mother was of royal blood, which qualified him for the Caledonian crown, should he be inclined to accept it. But the independent Picts were reluctant to place themselves under the rule of even their own kings, let alone those of other tribes. The notion of a Pictish King, ruling over a unified kingdom of all the Pictish tribes, was but a distant, future possibility.

Still, the popular opinion was that if there ever could be one Pictish king, Calach could be the one.

Calach had proven his bravery and prowess his entire life, both on hunts and on battlefields across the land. He was a defender of all Picts and a champion of Pictish independence. When marauders ventured west from the Nordic lands, as they often did, they were met with stiff resistance. Invariably, Calach was there to join the resistance and see that they were repelled.

He loved the Pictish ways. He cherished the culture they had developed and the respectful, diplomatic ways in which they normally dealt with one another. Calach would readily give his life for his people, should that ever be necessary.

Sioltach and the surviving Selgovae warriors knew the truth of that. They needed to reach Calach at all costs.

As the Selgovae riders made their way north, they were joined by other Selgovae from the northern reaches of their territory, and by others from the nearby Votadini and Novantii tribes. Word had spread quickly, and eager Picts across the land began to mobilize to join the resistance.

The leaders of each tribe set out for Muthill, the sacred council place in the heart of the Caledonii realm. All would seek united council, and all would seek an able leader, a great warrior, to unite them against the Roman incursion.

By the end of the third day after the atrocities at Balloch, all the tribal leaders had arrived at the Muthill council fire, near the seat of Pictish unity called Scone.

Melcon, the Caledonian king, called the council to order. He spoke first.

"Tell us of this atrocity, young Sioltach. Tell us everything you saw." Melcon and the other chiefs and elders settled in to hear Sioltach's account.

Sioltach remained visibly shaken, and he had trouble gathering his words. His lips quivered as he began.

"My wife…" Sioltach choked back his tears. He pointed solemnly to his closest friend. "His wife…his children…they're all dead. They were raped. Burned…"

Calach watched Sioltach closely from his position behind Melcon. He winced as he felt Sioltach's anguish. He tried hard to imagine what they had seen, but could not. He felt his heart filling with rage, and he restrained the urge to spring up and rush to revenge. Calach forced himself to sit quietly and wait for Sioltach to continue.

"These Romans are worse than we have heard," Sioltach continued. "We all know how they seduced the Pretani with promises of peace and civilized ways. They bought the Pretani with Roman citizenship and so-called high honors. The Pretani fell for the Roman seduction. Some of them walk around foolish and blind, wearing togas and speaking in the Latin tongue. They have not been treated badly, except for the loss of their freedom.

"I've sometimes wondered," said Creag, another Selgovae, "if maybe it wouldn't have been so bad for us to do the same, if only our freedom meant less to us. But by the gods, I'd never have it, and neither would any of you!" Creag gazed defiantly around the circle of faces.

Sioltach also looked around at his fellow tribesmen, with fury burning in his eyes.

"By the gods," Sioltach shouted, "I swear to you today that I'm glad for that. I will fight these inhuman pigs to the end of the earth!"

"As we all will, with you, by your side," shouted Drust, of the Venicones tribe. "Death to these invaders!" He looked around to supportive nods.

Other distraught Selgovae survivors related their own details of the terrible carnage, and the tribal leaders assessed the troubling developments. A pall fell over the gathering as the realization dawned that a lengthy era of peace and tranquility had suddenly ended.

"They killed the children," Sioltach continued. He began to break down again. "They raped our wives and daughters as they lay dying, and mothers as they screamed, watching their own babies cut in two or dashed against the rocks. Old men and women stood trembling, begging for just one more breath as their limbs were hacked away. I cannot tell you the extent of these monsters' cruelty, which I have seen with my own eyes. In my nightmares I could not have imagined these things. In our worst days we could not have done the likes of this."

"I watched them set fire to houses where people were hiding," Ranulf added. "They barred the doors, and then they laughed as the children screamed."

Sioltach began to speak, but he choked and could say no more. He sank trembling to the ground. A Caledonii couple sat and embraced the grieving man, in a futile attempt to comfort him.

Melcon sat in thought for a long moment. Then he raised his hand and spoke.

"Our course is clear," Melcon said. "We will all join the fight to defend the Selgovae, of course. In truth, we will be defending ourselves." He paused, as all those gathered nodded in agreement. "But this is a weighty problem to consider."

Melcon's look was solemn, his eyes grave.

"We all well know of Boudiccea's rebellion not so long ago," Melcon continued. "She led a fierce uprising, unmatched before or since. It was crushed. She may have come a breath away from victory, but in the end it mattered not. Far too many Romans came to replace those she destroyed. And now her Pretani are nothing but dogs on Roman leashes." Melcon paused as all considered his words. "We must carefully consider our course, that we do not follow the great Boudiccea into the dust."

The gathered warriors agreed, nodding and murmuring their assent. While they talked among themselves, Calach slid closer toward Melcon, and whispered for a long time into his ear. Sioltach watched intently from a short distance away. He prayed that Calach would support a united resistance, and that he would consent to lead it.

Sioltach would have been pleased to hear Calach's vigorous bid to do just that.

Brude of the Smertae also watched Calach from the shadows. His look betrayed something other than admiration or support.

When Calach finally pushed back from Melcon with a grim intensity in his eyes, Melcon stood and waited for the Picts to grow quiet. He nodded to the kings of the other nineteen tribes, seated in a circle around the council fire. The markings of wild beasts and mystical signs danced across their faces in the firelight. When the din settled into an expectant silence, Melcon extended his ornately tattooed arms and began to speak.

"My brothers and sisters, it is good that we are all here together in peace and support. It causes me indescribable pain that we are here under such dire circumstances. We have long lived in peace, with few exceptions of little consequence. We have fulfilled our ancestors' dreams here in this land, for untold years. We have much to defend, much we hold dear." He paused. "We are not like the Pretani," Melcon declared. Sioltach nodded his agreement. "We have no use for the Romans. They offer us nothing, but if we let them, they will take from us much."

The murmuring of the crowd grew louder, and more of those gathered nodded in enthusiastic agreement.

"We will repel these invaders," Melcon continued. "We all knew the day might come when the southern lands would not be enough for the Romans, and that they'd come for us. We've watched from the comfort of our highlands in the hope that we'd continue to escape their gaze. But they're too hungry. This day had to come. It was but a matter of time." He paused. "It's time. They have set their eyes upon us.

"Of course, none of us ever dreamed that this day would bring such unspeakable atrocity. Our enemy is ruthless and strong. We cannot rush into disorganized battle against this beast. Disunity will be our defeat. It is time for us to take unprecedented measures."

Melcon turned to look toward Calach, and then he turned back to the crowd.

"We must unite." Melcon continued. "As we all well know, for the Picts that is no easy task. As we also well know, we now have no other choice. We must cast aside, for a time, our distrust of leaders with too much power, over too many people. We must find it within ourselves to submit our tribal will to that of the greater good. In the past we could lend temporary support to one another in the defense of lesser threats. Today we must become one, at least for a time.

"The question, of course, is 'one what?' And under whom? Who will lead us as one, and to what extent will he lead us? When this war is won, what happens then? We must answer these questions, in a manner upon which we can all agree. We must do so now."

The wisdom of Melcon's words was evident. Melcon let the words sink in as all those gathered contemplated them in silence. Finally, Melcon spoke one last time.

"Our beloved Calach has given me his thoughts on this matter. I consider them to be worthy and wise. Calach has proven his honor and his courage in the defense of most of your tribes, at one time or another, against this foe or that. He has fought well by your sides, and he has always returned home to reclaim his peace. His ambitions are clear, and you know them to be pure. Hear him now, and decide for yourselves the merit of his words."

Melcon motioned to Calach, and then he returned to his seat by the fire.

Calach stood and walked close to the fire's edge. He stood quiet for a moment, looking around, seeking out the faces of those with whom he'd stood in the past, in defense of one another's interests against numerous enemies. He recognized countless friends, many of whom he considered to be brothers. His love for these people was evident.

Calach had the unusual ability to sense the emotions of those in his presence, and he stood for a moment absorbing those of this gathering of clans. He sensed an intense foreboding, and an unyielding resolve to stand united against a common enemy. It was that to which he spoke.

"My brothers, and my friends, I am both saddened and infuriated by this day's ruthless devastation," Calach began. "I cannot tell you the pain it brings to my heart to hear Sioltach's words, along with those of the others. I have spent many days with the Selgovae, and I cannot bear the loss of even one, let alone so many of them. Brothers and sisters have died today, and I want to make these Romans pay for that." A unanimous roar of assent went up throughout the gathering. Calach waited calmly for it to subside.

"It's clear that we face an enemy the likes of which we have never seen. It would be one thing to face an army of this size. It's yet another to face one so inhuman. We cannot risk losing our freedom to such demons.

"We must unite all of our warriors, to the last man and woman, into one Pictish army until we have vanquished this mortal enemy. It threatens us all. We should send all who cannot fight into the north, as far as possible, into the Lugii and the Cornavii lands. These Romans would kill them all if we allowed it. The innocent must remain safe, as much as our land must remain free."

Everyone listened attentively to Calach's call for an unprecedented confederation of their tribes.

"And I suppose it would be you who would lead this united army, Calach?" someone yelled from a distance away, in the shadows. It was Brude, a powerful and celebrated Smertae warrior.

Brude's jealousy of Calach was widely known. He was a fine fighter and a capable leader. Calach had always supported Brude, and had never tried to best him in front of his people. But many of the Smertae considered Calach a hero, and some Smertae children openly idolized him. While Calach was uncomfortable with such admiration, it irked

Brude to see it lavished so richly upon Calach rather than upon himself. Calach would prefer that the admiration of the Smertae people were reserved for Brude.

"I would not presume such an honor," Calach replied. "If we are to fight united, then we must choose a leader from among us, upon whom we can all agree, and to whom we can all commit our loyalty. I for one will follow any leader who is chosen by the twenty tribes, and I will follow that leader to the very ends of this earth."

There was silence. As Calach stood looking toward Brude, someone murmured Calach's name, and then repeated it. The lone voice was joined by a few, and then by a few more. In a moment, the murmur had grown into a chant, and thousands of Picts stood there in the night at Muthill, at the Council of All Picts, chanting the name of their new, unanimously chosen general.

"Calach! Calach! Calach!"

Calach raised his hand for silence. The chorus slowly faded. Calach struggled with his next words, as if he were reluctant to continue.

"I would accept the honor of leading our united army, but only if all of you would have it so." Calach looked purposely to Brude, who stood silent.

The sound of cheering, yelling, and war cries rang through the surrounding hills as thousands of Picts again voiced their unanimous approval. The roar evolved into a united chorus once again, chanting Calach's name.

Brude glared and turned away in disgust. His displeasure was not lost on Calach.

The kings and generals of each of the tribes approached Calach together to express their personal approval of his offer to lead them. It was a clear choice, and they all knew that the day the war was over Calach would relinquish this high honor and return home, content to live the hunter's life among his tribe.

8

Federation

THE KINGS AND THEIR GENERALS met well into the night, discussing the strategies, the goals, and the agreements that would bind and guide this new federation of Picts through the biggest war of their long and noble history. They were careful to craft a union that would only exist until it had served its express purpose.

Calach organized the Pictish armies into a well-trained and closely-knit force, one that would match Roman might with Pictish guile, and Roman greed with Pictish passion. The Picts would thwart any Roman attempt to subjugate them.

The first task for Calach's army was to assess the enemy, to learn how best to match their strengths and exploit their weaknesses. Calach selected the most elite of each tribe's warriors to form scouting units, and he sent emissaries to the south to recruit Pretani warriors who had lived among the Romans, and perhaps had fought alongside them, yet who held no loyalty toward them. Pretani recruits would provide considerable insight into Roman strength and tactics. They might also be eager for another opportunity to battle the empire that had enslaved them.

Calach's second task was to win Brude's support. Calach admired Brude, and he knew that he would need his help in leading an army bigger than any Pict had ever led. Calach also knew that the slightest division among the Picts would be disastrous.

Calach went to find Brude outside the tent of the Smertae delegation to the war council. Representatives from each tribe had come quickly to the Caledonii lands, and had brought only what they could gather on short notice. Brude was sitting by the fire watching several of his men as they prepared the evening meal. Brude seemed detached from those around him, lost in deep thought. Calach sat beside him without a word.

Brude glanced sideways toward Calach. He shook his head slightly and gave an irritated huff. Calach looked directly at Brude, waiting for him to say what was on his mind. Calach sensed frustration and jealousy, and he knew he'd have to deal with Brude carefully to gain his support.

"Why are you here with me? Do you not have celebrating to do? Or is it gloating that suits you more?" Brude asked in disgust.

"Gloating? Why would I gloat?" Calach asked.

"Be serious, man. You've just been chosen High King of the Picts."

"King? I think not. There is no King of the Picts."

"Not yet, there isn't. But I've no doubt there will be one day. And who do you think will be the one to wear that crown when that day comes?"

"I already have my king," said Calach. "And you have yours. I will not be anybody's king. I'm a hunter, a warrior, and a husband. That is more than enough for me."

Brude turned to face Calach. He studied Calach's eyes intently.

"You say that now," Brude finally said. "Wait until you return from war victorious. You heard them tonight. They worship you, Calach. They will make you their king. You will not refuse. Why would you?"

"I won't have to. My own people would not choose me to be their king. That is because they well know my heart. I wish to be king no more than you wish to be a goat." Calach looked intently at Brude, and then continued, "No, Brude, I want to be no man's king. I have no desire for such an honor. It would please me well to see the Caledonii kingship go to my brother, Gabhran. He is the popular choice, and he is my choice, and for good reason. He would be a fine king. I would give my life for him. Besides, I know of no Caledonii alive who wants to see a king over all the Picts.

"Brude, you must know this: I wish only to live a good life, and to live it in freedom. I would take one good day in Fiona's arms over a lifetime as king of the world." Brude gave out a long and hearty laugh.

"Then you are a damned fool!" Brude said. "If you were a king, you could have a dozen Fiona's."

"I only want one Fiona," Calach said. He stood and turned to face Brude. "And I only want one man to stand by my side and help me to lead this army." Brude stopped laughing and looked straight up into Calach's eyes, his own eyes narrowing as if to make out some tiny thing. W*hy would Calach choose me?* he wondered. *Is this some sort of trick?*

"You want me to be your number two." Brude said it with contempt, but also with a hint of surprise. "Why me? Surely you must think there are better men."

"I want you to be my second in command. You're a good man, Brude. One of the very best. I need your support. Our people have asked me to lead our army. No one has ever led a united army of all the Pictish tribes. You are a fine warrior, one of the finest I've ever known, and I will need your help."

Brude considered Calach's words. His pride made it difficult for him to subordinate himself to the younger man. When asked, he would say that Calach's youthful exuberance was the cause for his disdain. But in the depths of his heart he knew that his resentment was far less dignified. He knew that what he really wanted was to *be* Calach, to enjoy the same inherent skill, and to command the same high regard in which his own Smertae people held Calach. Brude knew that that would never be so, and he hated Calach for that.

"Your number two," Brude repeated. He seemed to be accepting the idea, with reluctance. "I will help you to lead this army? You believe that I have something to offer you?"

"Of course I do," Calach exclaimed. "I've fought beside you enough, my friend, to know how capable you are. You have a fine eye for strategy, and the quick wit for tactics. You're one of the fiercest warriors I know. As the gods well know, I'd not want to be your enemy!"

Brude took a brief moment to contemplate those last few words, and then he stood and extended his hand. "Then count me as your friend, and your number two," Brude said. "It is done!"

"My second in command," Calach repeated, correcting Brude again. Calach grasped Brude's hand firmly.

"Till the end of this war," Brude added.

"Till the end," Calach repeated. He beamed at Brude. "Together, we will win this thing, my brother!"

9

Fiona

CALACH STARED into the fire outside the small house he shared with Fiona, his wife and the love of his life. He had a lot to think about, and a lot of things to settle in his heart. So much had happened, and so quickly, that Calach struggled to absorb all of it. In the past, invaders had come in manageable numbers, and the tribe closest to the assault would send riders to rally their neighbors' support. The invaders were usually easily repelled, and everything returned quickly to normal.

But this time things were different. The massive Roman forces surpassed any previous invasion, and the brutality at Balloch was staggering. Calach truly feared for the security of all that he held dear.

"Are you all right, love?" Fiona's soft voice broke his reverie. Calach looked up at Fiona with a small grin.

"Just thinking, that's all."

"About the Romans?"

"About you." He reached up and took her hand, pulling her close. "You're everything to me, Fiona."

"As you are to me, Calach."

"I want forever with you. I will not let these Romans take that from me."

"Nor will I," proclaimed Fiona.

Calach was silent for a moment. His thoughts shifted to Brude.

"I asked Brude to be my second in command," he said.

"A good, but curious choice," Fiona replied. "I'd have thought you'd have chosen Gabhran. I'm surprised." She paused. "Why Brude?"

"Unity. I will need to unite these tribes in battle, Fiona. They must see this as the alliance that it is, and not as a Caledonii army that they have joined. With Brude as second in command, it will be clear. Besides, it is important to me that no harm comes to Gabhran. He would make for the Caledonii tribe an excellent king, and Melcon is growing old. If it is the will of the tribe, I want to see Gabhran as the next Caledonii king. I will see that he is kept from harm. I cannot say that to him, but I will do all that it takes to make it so."

Calach kept his next thought private. He intended to gain Gabhran's solemn oath that he would hold Fiona's safety as his personal and sacred duty through each battle, until the last was finished.

"It is wise for you to keep that idea from Gabhran's ears," Fiona said. "He would be most displeased." She paused. "You're too protective, Calach. I hope you have no such foolish thoughts regarding me. I assure you, I can fend for myself." Her eyes blazed.

"Oh, I know you can! I wouldn't think of overprotecting you, my love," he lied. He swore to himself. She always saw through him so easily. He struggled to find the words that would convince her not to join the war against the Romans, but he fully expected that his efforts would be futile.

"I know," Calach continued awkwardly, "that you are among the most able of Caledonii archers."

Fiona raised an eyebrow and flashed him look. She knew from his tone the direction those words were headed, and her look warned him clearly not to pursue it.

"I am," she agreed firmly.

"And I know that you can best any man with a sword or a well-balanced pike."

Fiona stood to her full height.

"Husband, I could best most men with nothing but a clumsy tree branch," she declared defiantly.

"Aye," Calach agreed. "That you could." He hesitated. "What I really would like say, dear wife, is that perhaps you might consider–"

"Consider *what*," Fiona demanded, turning to face Calach with her hands firmly on her hips. "Which bow to bring with me into battle? Which sword to strap to my side?"

Calach looked away. After a moment he drew a deep sigh and continued.

"I don't want you hurt," he finally said, with a hint of resignation. "Or worse."

"Nor I you," Fiona countered. "And how is that any different? Do you think I worry less about you? You would have me sit here and wait for news of you, to spare yourself the possibility of receiving news of me? And you think that fair?"

Calach shook his head.

"It's just that I love you so," he pleaded. "I don't want to place you in danger."

"We are all in danger, no matter where we are, when our people are under attack," Fiona retorted, her voice growing sharp. "And you did not put any of us there!" Calach listened quietly. "You would have me wait here for our warriors to fall, so that our enemies may come and take me as they please? No, Calach. That is not our way. You know that. You have always known that."

"Yes," Calach agreed. He had always known that. Before they were married Fiona had firmly declared her intention to be one of the finest warriors in the land.

Pictish women enjoyed the same rights as men to choose their fate, and if they chose to fight as warriors, then they would fight as warriors. The Picts drew no distinctions between men and women in that regard. Calach was wrong to ask this of her, and he knew it.

Fiona was an exceptional archer, and she could handle a horse better than most. Mounted archers were highly esteemed in the Pictish armies. Fiona had proven herself in battle, just weeks after her seventeenth birthday, when the Danes launched another raid on the eastern coast. She insisted on joining the defense, and she returned to the village a celebrated warrior after the battle was won. Calach himself had etched her victory tattoo above her left breast: an ornate eagle with its talons outstretched, above the prone figure of a man, her fallen foe.

Calach had often struggled to resolve his love and concern for Fiona with his admiration and respect for her superior skills as a warrior.

"I don't care if I am wrong," Calach insisted. His voice rose uncharacteristically. "I do not want you hurt. You are my wife, and I forbid you to fight!"

Calach turned to face Fiona, and he was startled by the equally uncharacteristic fury that blazed in her eyes.

"You have no right," she seethed. "And you know that better than anyone."

"And I want you to live," Calach hissed through clenched teeth.

Calach and Fiona glared at one another for a long silence. The tension between them reverberated in the air. Calach's shoulders heaved, and he was unaware that his fists were tightly clenched, his knuckles white. Fiona stood firm, feet wide, and her hands on her hips, fuming.

Suddenly, Calach's shoulders relaxed, and he sat on a nearby log.

"I love you too much," he said, turning to face her, his eyes softening, "I don't know what I would do if I lost you."

Fiona softened slightly in turn. She moved slowly toward Calach, her eyes still hard and unrelenting, and she reached her hand toward his.

"I am a warrior," she insisted, "just like you. I cannot sit idle as our people go to battle. I must be there with my bow, and my sword, and my heart, and my strength. I must repel these invaders just as surely as you must, or I will not be who I am."

"I will ask you one more time, because I must," Calach said, with only a hint of resignation. "Please stay home this time."

"And I will answer you one more time, because you ask yet again. I will fight by your side, in the Pictish way. Our way is our strength, and it will be our victory. My strength will add to our strength. I will be a part of your army, and I will be part of its certain victory."

Calach shook his head in frustration and turned his face away.

Fiona did not acknowledge the single tear she saw lingering at the corner of his averted eye.

"I will return victorious by your side," she softly assured him.

"And if you don't?"

"I will," Fiona insisted.

"No! Please! Do not do this, just this one time. Please, Fiona!"

Fiona crossed her arms in stubborn refusal. Calach stood and stormed away in frustration and nagging fear.

Calach roamed for hours through the darkness of the shadows of Muthill. His fear was inexplicable, and he was overcome by an intense and unbearable foreboding that had filled his heart. He was driven as never before to prevent Fiona from taking part in the battle against the Romans.

At long last, Calach returned to Fiona. He stood for a moment in the shadows watching her as she sat at the edge of the fire deep in thought. He was certain she did not yet know he was there. He wanted to watch her this way until the end of time, sitting in the firelight in the night. Calach could love nothing more than he did her.

"Your reasoning for Brude as your second is sound," Fiona suddenly said, without looking up. Calach was startled, and impressed. She had heard his approach from far off. She did indeed possess the skills of a warrior. "I can see the wisdom of the choice, as will everyone else," she continued. "It is small wonder that so many are so willing to support you."

The Pictish nature was to give only grudging support to their leaders, lest their leaders grow full of their power over men. The support that the Picts had expressed for Calach earlier in the night was unprecedented.

Calach moved to sit beside his wife. He placed a tender arm around her broad, slender shoulders. Fiona leaned into him.

Calach's thoughts had turned to another issue. He thought deeply for a long moment before he spoke more quietly, and anxiously.

"I said earlier that I want revenge," he said. Fiona nodded silently, listening. "The moment I spoke those words, my father's voice, and the voice of another, echoed in my ear from long ago. Do you remember our first day, after the hunt?"

Fiona smiled, her eyes sparkling with the memory.

"How could I forget?" she asked.

Calach's thoughts drifted back to that happiest of days, when he first set his eyes upon Fiona. It had been his third successful hunt, at the age of twelve. His father's hunting party was returning from the hunt, during which Calach had killed a wild boar. His face and body were painted with woad and ash, and the blood from the kill was still drying on his hands and arms. He'd received his first tattoo, of which he was exceedingly proud. It was an etching of a wild beast, on the left side of his chest, below his collarbone. Calach had imagined himself to be quite an impressive sight.

Fiona's extended family, of the Creones tribe to the north, had entered the Caledonii village from the north just as the hunting party arrived from the east. Calach's eyes were immediately drawn to the beautiful young girl among the visitors.

She was younger than Calach. Her auburn hair was long and thick, and her brilliant green eyes radiated intelligence and warmth. She carried herself like a warrior princess, Calach thought. He could not take his eyes off of her.

The hunters laughed as Calach stood dumbstruck. His father slapped him on the back roughly, bidding the others to look upon how his beloved son had grown into a man.

As the hunters dragged their kill to the village center, Fiona and her family drew near. She was as transfixed by Calach as he was by her, although she thought to herself that he was indeed a frightful sight in blood and woad. She had also admired his new tattoo, not yet fully healed.

"You were so charming," Fiona reminded him, "telling us that we were to join your family for dinner that night." Calach had phrased the question more as an abrupt and hopeful statement than as an invitation. His father had shot him a stern look, thinking him brash.

"I was being hospitable," Calach protested. Fiona laughed.

"You were being love struck," she retorted. "It was so endearing. You lost your manners to your youthful heart."

Calach smiled sheepishly.

"My heart is still youthful," he said. He grinned and winked suggestively.

"After the meal was finished," Calach said, "I was so excited, telling and retelling the story of how I killed that wild boar. I wanted you to see that I was a great hero."

"I did. You were," beamed Fiona. "To me, you've always been."

"Well, later that night, my father pulled me aside. He said something to me that I have never forgotten, and never will." Calach paused for a long moment. "My father said to me, 'son, we do not celebrate the hunt because we have killed an animal. We celebrate because we have fed our clan.' He asked me if I understood the difference. I did.

"He then told me that good men do battle only to protect the things they love, and not simply to defeat other men. My father said that if I should ever find myself going to battle for revenge, or for glory, and not for the defense of the things all men should cherish, then I should know that day that I had become a lesser man."

"Your father was wise."

"But I feel only vengeance in my heart this day, Fiona. I'm struggling to put it down. There are a dozen reasons to fight the Romans, but in my heart right now the desire for vengeance is the only one I see. I fear that if I let this vengeance drive me, it will weaken me, and make me a lesser man."

Fiona looked at Calach tenderly. "It's a reasonable thing you feel. It's an unheard thing, what they did to that defenseless Selgovae village. We all feel the rage, Calach." She slid her arms about his waist. "I want revenge, too."

Finally, Calach said "I must keep my mind free of revenge if I am to see clearly and lead well. I know we will not beat the Romans with force. They outnumber us and are much better armed. If I give in to rage, I may begin to use force instead of tactics and cunning. I suspect I will need your help in this."

"And you'll have it, of course, as always. You will be fine, my love. You will do well. Your heart is strong enough to choose right over wrong, and not lose your way. You've never let me down before."

She nudged him gently, smiling into his eyes. "Stop worrying, and join me…" Fiona rose and walked backwards, slowly, toward the door to their house. She loosed her hair seductively, and then quietly disappeared within. Calach followed without delay.

10

Watching

IN THE COLD GRAY OF DAWN, Calach's narrowed eyes blazed at the sight of Roman invaders in his land. He studied the enemy intently through the wet, black trees. He had been studying them for days, assessing their strengths, and more importantly, tallying their weaknesses. He knew they were far from home, and he could tell by the apparent disposition of the soldiers that they were not the elite. He suspected, then, that their empire was facing bigger battles elsewhere, and that this was the best they could send to Calach's remote land – a decided advantage for Calach and the Picts.

Besides, Calach thought, *one brave Pict is far more powerful than a thousand of these would-be conquerors.* Indeed, at that moment, Calach felt that the courage and resolve that pounded in his own heart dwarfed the shivering host assembled in the valley below.

But there are so many, he thought. The practical mind of a general had intervened. The Picts were truly far outnumbered. Calach could not possibly realize that he was facing a full tenth of the entire Roman army. He was a much bigger quarry than he knew. He winced as he calculated their numbers, estimating that he was outnumbered by at least ten to one, at least until reinforcements began to arrive from the northern tribes.

Calach had never seen an army so large, or so well armed. He knew that he had no choice but to attack as soon as possible, and hope for adequate reinforcements from the twenty tribes. Gabhran and Fiona were leading the recruitment effort to the farthest reaches of the land, and Calach anticipated a steady flow of warriors to the fight.

Calach was a brilliant tactician, a noble leader, and a fearless warrior. The gods had blessed his Caledonii tribe with the finest army in the land. Among the other tribes, the Caledonii were widely regarded as elite among the Picts. Calach had led his men and women into battle against the best, and in his victories he had forged alliances with his fiercest opponents. Some even called the whole of the island "Calach's Land," though that was certainly an exaggeration, he thought with a grin. He didn't want the whole island. He only wanted his tiny part of it, surrounded by the land and the people he loved, and with Fiona standing proudly at his side.

But now he was being drawn into a war he didn't choose, by an invader that had no business threatening his people's home.

So, these are the Romans, he thought, as he studied them. Calach had heard tales of Roman conquest, and of the glory of the Roman Empire. *Impressive indeed.*

He couldn't really blame the nations that had joined the Empire in relief after losing their terrible wars. But it wasn't in the Pictish blood, either to lose, or to join should they be vanquished. Calach knew that in the event of defeat, Picts would resist and rebel to the bitter end, until every last one of them was dead. There would be no easy victory over the Picts, and no subsequent joyous assimilation.

Roman strategy relied heavily upon brute force, and upon their strength in numbers. They had often conquered nations not with superior skill, but by throwing legion after legion into the war until the enemy were ultimately overpowered. They replenished their losses by absorbing what was left of the conquered army.

This was an incredible weakness of the Roman army, Calach thought. The captive soldier fighting to prolong his conquered existence, or the soldier fighting for the glory and honor of his emperor, were cripples against a warrior fighting for the freedom of his people. Calach had long been taught the Pictish belief that a freedom fighter fights with the strength of ten men – five of his father's fathers, and five of the sons of his sons.

Calach perceived other Roman weaknesses, too, in the very battle tactics that were their strength. One of the great weaknesses of an army entrenched in conventional battle tactics was exposed when that army faced an unconventional enemy. Calach's tactics were anything but conventional, even by Pictish tribal standards. Calach had demonstrated considerable genius in countless battles, not only against other Picts, but also more often against foreign invaders from the south and the east.

The Picts would not meet the Romans on the field. They would stage sporadic raids against the Roman encampments, changing tactics as needed, and capitalizing on the Romans' unfamiliarity with the terrain, the climate, and the Picts themselves. They would also throw the Romans off guard by attacking them in their very position of strength: within their own fortifications. Calach suspected the Romans would be less effective fighting in close quarters than they would be on an open field. Calach would also make good use of the Roman soldiers' fear of the unknown.

Something seemed odd to Calach as he studied the army stretched out across the boggy plain before him. He sensed a subtle, hidden weakness. Somehow he sensed that the Picts had a better chance of defeating this Roman Legion than it would seem, but he couldn't quite put his finger on what it was that made it so.

Suddenly, something happened that made it clear to him. The first light of dawn was just beginning to break over the eastern hills. He was watching as two Roman soldiers gathered wood just beyond the edge of the clearing, acting casual, almost nonchalant. But their nervousness could not be masked. They stole brief glances around them, into the woods, into the hills. They talked to one another in a hush, and gave an occasional nervous laugh.

And then they nearly jumped out of their skins when the crack of a twig rang out from the trees to Calach's right; a deer had approached the tree line at the edge of the bog. Calach had known for some time that the deer was there, just beyond his sight. He'd sensed its presence by instinct, mostly, but also from the gentle rustling sound of smaller game moving away from the deer. One could also always safely assume that deer were close by, especially at this time of the morning.

The two soldiers froze for a moment, much longer than Calach thought normal for someone startled by a deer. He almost laughed out loud at the sight. But he didn't. He pondered the peculiarity of their fear. It was most unbecoming of the hardened soldiers of a great Roman Empire. He began to suspect that numbers were to be his enemy's only advantage. But he wouldn't underestimate them just the same. That was to be one of *his* advantages.

As the sun rose higher and warmed the ground, the pall of fear almost perceptibly rose from the Roman camp along with the evaporating dew. Calach and his scouts retreated into the deep wood. They didn't make a sound.

11

Battle Plan

"THERE SURE ARE A LOT of them. And they seem very serious about this." Ailpein looked upon the Roman camp in dismay.

"They're very well armed."

"Twelve thousand Roman soldiers, at least…"

"We're so far outnumbered. How will we stand against them?"

Calach's battle-hardened face was grave and silent as he considered his scouts' observations of the Roman legion. He watched the others as they, too, listened intently. He could feel their apprehension. While he didn't want anyone to underestimate the invaders before them, he also knew the value of hope and optimism.

"They've conquered a lot of other lands, with armies far bigger than ours," said the dark-haired Ailpein. "How could *we* hope to stop them when no one else could?"

Ailpein was no coward. He was one of the bravest of warriors, and one of the noblest of his clan. Calach saw immense strength in Ailpein, and he could see Ailpein's line rising to great honor long after he was gone. Calach had a special affection for Ailpein and his small family.

"But they are not united, even in their own close ranks," Calach said softly, barely above a whisper. His warriors looked up at him in unison, listening.

"Look at them. Really look at them. Some of those soldiers are Romans citizens far from home, both new recruits and battle-weary veterans. But most of them are a patchwork of conscripts and slaves from decimated nations and trampled tribes. Ambitious young Romans who were born into affluence are thrown in with unruly soldiers who were sent to the front for reasons we can only guess, and they bunk together with the remnants of armies they've defeated." Calach paused to let his men consider his points.

"I think that this army before us is motivated by a mix of avarice, fear, defeat, and the simple need to survive their circumstances. They are here to expand a great and glorious domain already stretched taut from its fortified, golden heart to the darkest misty edges of its reach. We, my noble warriors, are the mist at the edge of that reach. And they, my dearest brothers, are not the best of Rome, or they would not be here with us.

"Look upon them. They have none of the passion that burns in your hearts. They are childless, wifeless, orphans far from home. They don't fight for family, for nation, or for ideals. They fight because they are told to fight or die. They are here to take lands they do not own, in the name of the very men who took their land and made them slaves.

"These slaves either long to be free again, or are already dead. It will be upon you to either set them free or make their death real. Those that would be free again are your brothers in arms. They will even the field."

Calach was silent now for a long time. Everyone thought hard on his words. As they sunk in, heads began to nod and eyes began to brighten. Calach could feel the mood and he knew he had won the first part of this battle, in the hearts of his men.

He finished, "these soldiers are in this fight only to stretch an empire over our graves. We will be fighting for our lives, for the love of our families, and for the freedom of our children's children. This battle will be ours."

Calach put his plan into motion. He found Morbet, the old musician. Morbet was brilliant with Pictish pipes. He produced the finest pipes that sounded hauntingly like human voices. Played together, they could produce the most beautiful and surreal sounds, like a chorus of angels. Considering the effect those pipes had always had on him, Calach imagined the effect they would have on the Romans, who had never before heard any sound quite like them.

"Pipes?" asked Morbet. "You want pipes?"

"Hundreds of them," said Calach.

"Pipes," repeated Morbet, nodding, confused.

"Pipes. And in your pipes I want you to capture all the voices of our ancestors, long gone." Domhnall looked curiously at Calach, his closest friend. Calach must have an interesting plan. He had a brilliant mind, and often came up with innovative strategies in hunts and in battle. Domhnall delighted in hearing his plans.

"A haunting sound that would be," Domhnall said.

"Imagine it," Calach said. "Imagine that you are a Roman soldier. You grew up in a sunny Mediterranean town, in the luxury of the greatest empire the world has known. You're surrounded by civilization and comforts, warmth and pleasures. The dark of night is filled with unbroken peace and security. You sleep softly, and always without fear.

"Now imagine that you find yourself on the edge of your civilization, where it's not so sunny, and not nearly so warm. There's darkness, and a mist the likes of which you've never seen, not even in the darkened forests of the Germanic lands. *This place must be haunted*, you might think to yourself. *I can't see the enemy, but I think he must surely be watching me.* It must be an unnerving thing.

"And now you lay there sleeping, or trying to, in the dead of night. The warmth of home is a distant memory, and the starkness of this place is an icy blanket over you. And then you hear the sound. It's distant at first, but then nearer, and nearer still. You can't place the sound; it's not human. *It must be ghosts,* you think. *Are my enemies already ghosts? Or are they demons. . ."*

Domhnall imagined it, and nodded enthusiastically.

"They'll be afraid," Domhnall said.

"Yes," said Calach. "I can only imagine it, but I suspect they will be intimidated. And the conquered slave-soldiers are mostly superstitious tribesmen from across the empire. They'll spook easier than the Romans."

"It's a good plan, Calach."

"It's a good plan," echoed Morbet. "I'll get to work."

12

Ghost Attack

THE MOON WAS STILL HIGH, and wispy, fleeting clouds crossed its face, casting eerie shadows across the land. Felix shifted uneasily in his bed. The damp air irritated him, and the cold seeped into his bones.

He had awoken anxious from a troubling dream. In his dream he lay paralyzed in the middle of a field of mud, the suction of the mud pulling him down into the earth. In the moonlit sky above him, the faces of demons swirled darkly, sneering down at him in contempt. They were speaking to him in a harsh, whispery language he didn't understand, but their meaning was clear. They were laughing at his impending death. Their words were a quiet, low-pitched howl that brought goose bumps to his skin and froze his blood. He felt his heart freezing solid as his breath caught in his tightening throat. These were the ghosts of evil men, or demons that would wipe him from the Earth. His fear grew more intense until it shook him from the dream.

And now he lay shivering in his bed, cursing the fate that brought him to this god-forsaken land. He'd imagined his service as a Roman soldier would be glorious, with heroic battles fought and won, and grand moments basking in the warmth of Roman victory. His dreams of building the empire on the ashes of barbarian tribes seemed a distant memory, as he lay here in this cold, damp place. He tried to think of better days, and to imagine better things to come. This hell could not last forever.

Or could it, he thought in contempt. This soldier's life was nothing like what he had dreamed it would be. He'd begun to think it would only be the death of him.

And then he heard it again. Felix glanced around the tent to see if the other soldiers had heard it too. They were all asleep. It was the faintest sound at first, from far off in the hills surrounding the Roman camp. With a start, Felix realized the sound in his dream had been real. It was a solemn, mournful moan. It grew louder and seemed to be coming closer to the camp. But then, just as it seemed upon him, it suddenly stopped.

After a dozen heartbeats, it started again. It was higher pitched now, and coming from the opposite side of the valley, coming closer to the camp by the second. Maybe it was different from the first, he thought. Then he was sure, because the first sound droned again from the original direction, picking up where it had stopped, and still approaching.

There were two plaintive moans now, each echoing its unique sound through the valley from the depths of the surrounding mountains.

And then there were three. Then a fourth joined in.

Lucius, Felix's boyhood friend, lay trembling in his own tent closer to the edge of camp. He had the same impression that Felix had, that these were demons soaring toward the Roman camp from different directions, and multiplying by the minute. The sounds were eerie, as if the voices of ghosts or demons, threatening. Like Felix, Lucius lay silent and still, with the same fear pounding in his chest.

Soon there were too many to count, dreadful demons flying and turning in the air above them, screaming and echoing out into the surrounding hills. In the darkness, Felix again saw the faces from his dream. He knew that they were there above the dense fabric of his tent, leering down upon him with their snarling, curled lips. They were real!

The moaning continued for what seemed hours. Lucius knew that he should get up and go outside, and face whatever enemy this was, like a good Roman soldier should. But he was frozen in his bed, paralyzed by his fear. Glancing nervously at his comrades, he saw that they were all, with the exception of Livius, wide-awake and motionless, terrified as he.

Lucius heard a rustling sound outside the tent. He wondered if the demons would come inside. He eyed his sword, but he realized that it would probably do him little good. His left hand inched toward it, nonetheless. He was sure now that there was movement outside. As he strained to identify the sound, a shadow caught his eye on the other side of the tent. He turned to look and came face to face with the most terrifying sight he'd ever seen.

There was a demon in the form of a wild man standing over Lucius, staring down at him with wide and menacing eyes. Its skin was a bluish gray, and covered with pictures of forms he couldn't identify. The wild, glaring eyes, deep-set in an oddly painted face, were framed by a massive mane of thick, wild hair. The demon lifted his forefinger to his lips as if to caution silence, and the face broke into a wide, maniacal grin.

Before Lucius knew it had happened, a strong dark hand covered his nose and mouth, while another closed around his voiceless throat, clamping it to the bed. Lucius felt the demon's hot breath on the clammy skin of his face, and the demon shifted its weight onto Lucius's body, holding him down. Lucius was seized with panicky terror as he realized he was about to die. Minutes began to drag as the infernal howling filled his ears and his lungs began to ache, and then to scream for air.

Lucius tried frantically to look for his comrades, to find out why they weren't coming to his aid. Just before his peripheral vision faded, he understood. He briefly saw them all, each with his own personal demon, each being pressed into his bed, each weighed down as his own blue demon snuffed the life from his body.

Lucius's vision narrowed to a point. All he could see now was the angry, leering, bizarrely painted blue face staring deeply into his dying eyes. The demon spoke to him then, in a deep and menacing voice. It was a language he didn't understand, but somehow the meaning was clear. Lucius knew as the world went black that this legion of Roman soldiers was face to face with the most terrible enemy any of them had ever seen.

A short distance away, Felix heard a rustling sound outside his tent. He wondered if the demons would come inside. He thought the sound might be soldiers, up to investigate the eerie moaning sound. He began to move slightly, as if to get up and join them, even as something inside him was pulling him back. He overcame the fear and swung his legs over the edge of the bed. He began to rise, staring intently at the door to the outside.

Suddenly, as quickly as the sound had come, it vanished. The wailing stopped, echoing away into the distance, and the rustling he'd thought he'd heard was also gone. He could hear his heart pounding in his ears, and he realized he was drenched in a cold sweat. After a moment, he lay back down, and began to try to quiet his pounding heart. And he began to pray for dawn.

13

Aftermath

DAWN CAME, and Felix drifted out of a fitful half-sleep. He heard shouts from all around the camp, and he warily shifted his legs to climb out of his bed. He threw on his tunic, strapped on his sword, and exited the tent.

The sight that greeted his bleary eyes stunned him. Soldiers were dragging lifeless bodies out of tents everywhere. He saw Antonius, a captain, striding angrily from tent to tent, assessing what had happened in the night. He cursed loudly at every corpse he discovered. Soldiers moved in and out of tents, dazed.

"Tally the dead!" shouted Antonius. "Centurions, report to me! What has happened here?" Antonius, a Centurion of the First Cohort, was in command of the situation, but even his eyes showed a glint of confused fear.

When the counting was done, there were more than three hundred dead. There was no sign of injury or violence to any of them. It was as if they had simply expired in the night, asphyxiating in their sleep. *The demons*, Felix thought, *came howling into the midst of our Legion,*

killing entire contubernia – tents with eight men each –
indiscriminately and with impunity.

The confusion quickly built into an uproar, as dazed soldiers
wandered through the camp trying to grasp what had happened, and
frantic centurions tried desperately to gain control.

Aquila, the camp Prefect, emerged from the command tent and
stormed into the center of the camp.

"Come to order!," Aquila bellowed. "Centurions, get your men in
order!"

The sight of Aquila had a quieting effect on the chaos. Men
automatically gravitated toward their cohorts to line up in formation at
his command. Centurions scurried to take charge of their men. As
order returned, Aquila gazed at the bodies gathered in front of the tents
in which they had died. He surveyed the disquieted troops and
struggled to make sense of what had happened.

Meanwhile, the band of Picts had gathered back at their camp, and
sat discussing the night's resounding success. It had been a small
detachment, only two hundred warriors and a band of twenty scouts.
The scouts had slipped silently over the wall and taken out the sentries
at the gate. In the shadows, they stripped the dead and donned their
uniforms and weapons, and then quietly opened the gates. Calach and
his men slipped into the camp just as the first pipe sounded, executed
the assault, and were gone long before any Roman realized they'd been
attacked.

"It was a thing of beauty, it was!" exclaimed Ailpein.

"Aye, it was," echoed Domhnall. "The pipers did the trick! It was
brilliant." He beamed at Calach. The effect of the pipes on the Romans
was exactly as Calach had planned, providing cover for the raid. The
Romans who awoke had lain frozen with fear in their beds.

The overzealous Picts could not resist the urge to overkill during
this attack. The plan had been for each of the two hundred warriors to
take one Roman life. But over three hundred soldiers had been killed.

Calach did not reprimand their overzealousness, but he quietly reminded them that success would always depend on each attack being carried out exactly as planned. Improvisation could result in grave mistakes, he cautioned.

Calach was greatly encouraged by the success of this first raid. Soon, after first light, his small detachment would return to report to the others its effect on the Romans.

"Three hundred twenty soldiers killed!" Quintus was furious. He stormed around the camp, eyeing the dead and sputtering in anger. "Three hundred twenty men are dead, and not a glimpse of who did this? Not a dagger lifted in defense? How could this be?" he demanded. Quintus glared at his troops. He could not imagine how anyone could slip into the midst of a Roman legion and wreak such destruction unchallenged, much less unnoticed. The Roman soldiers slept eight men per tent. Forty tents had been wiped out without a sound.

Well, not exactly without a sound, Quintus had to admit. Quintus had been shaken by the ghostly sounds just like everyone else. He had witnessed some incredible things in his years of conquest, but never anything that had compared with what happened last night. Few things had stricken him with fear like that. But Quintus could not let his men see his fear.

He repeated, "three hundred twenty Roman soldiers slaughtered in their beds! Centurions, you will meet with me in the command tent and explain this to me, each of you. This will not be permitted to happen again!"

Inside the command tent, under the intense gaze of their Prefect, the centurions struggled to grasp what had happened in the night. What kind of enemy was this they faced? Even the fiercest Germanic barbarians had never dared to set foot inside a Roman camp. Now it appeared the camp had been ravaged by ghosts in the night. Who else but ghosts would dare such a thing? Lesser armies quaked at the very sight of a Roman legion. Surely this act could not have been perpetrated by mere mortals.

They had all heard the sounds, of course, but none could come up with a suitable explanation for what it was. No instrument they knew could make such a sound. It was no human or animal sound, either. Demons were the only explanation. Demons had struck at their very heart in the dark of night.

The centurion Varius ventured, "We have seen no enemy – only the evidence of one – in the weeks that we have been marching north. The land has appeared so far to be desolate and uninhabited. We would have seen a human enemy with the strength to attack us like this."

"We've not seen so much as a sign of human life since we left that village. Only wildlife and the damnable mist," said Septimus.

"Even the signposts we came across at the beginning of the march pointed to empty valleys and clearings, as if the villages have long disappeared," Varius said. "I know it's not possible, but it looks like it was demons that attacked us. What else could it have been?"

Quintus could barely mask his troubled thoughts. He had heard nothing in the night besides the infernal moaning as it covered the camp in fear. He alone had rushed outside his tent to investigate. The sound stopped abruptly the moment he exited the tent, as if it had sensed his presence. It resumed in a moment, then it was joined by the others, and they seemed to be focused on his presence. Seeing no one else outside, he had returned to his tent in a fear he could never reveal to his troops. Nothing in his long years of battle had prepared him for that experience, and now it was all he could do to swallow the shame he felt over his failure to confront it.

As the centurions struggled with their speculations, Quintus struggled with his thoughts. He suddenly rose and waved the centurions to silence.

"We will not know this today. We can only guess and grasp at straws. Rally the men, and calm them. Put down any supernatural fears, and minimize this in their eyes. Prepare the dead for burning, and make it quick.

"Send out scouts to find this enemy. Put a face on him.

"You will ensure that the legion is more prepared this coming night to face another attack, with their swords and not with silence. Report back to me after noon."

Quintus turned his back on the centurions, which was their signal to leave him alone. Once alone, he sank into contemplation of this bizarre development.

14

Second Attack

"WE TOOK A GOOD BITE out of the beast," Ailpein laughed. "They won't forget it any time soon!" It had been three days since the first attack, and the warriors were growing restless for another go. The Romans had moved another thirty miles north, and set up a stronger fortification than the one Calach's band had attacked. In the mean time, more Picts had arrived from the north to swell the army's ranks.

Domhnall asked, "Will we follow the same plan again, Calach?"

"No," Calach answered. "This time will be a little different. After the last raid the Romans will associate the pipes with an attack. This time we attack in silence, quietly in and out, before the pipes begin. At the start of the pipes, the soldiers will come to arms. But they'll find no enemy to fight, for we'll be long gone into the night. They'll never see the ghosts who slew their soldiers once again, this time while they stood ready."

The strategy was a good one, the warriors agreed. The Romans would discover the dead after the pipes stopped. They would think their men were killed during the piping, and it would appear to them that an invisible enemy had carried out the attack before their very eyes.

"Remember, though, to follow the plan exactly," Calach cautioned again. "Timing is critical! We must all be back from the tents before the piping begins. We will add drums for this attack. The first beating of the *bodhrán* will be the signal to move out of the Roman camp. Finish your work by that time, and leave immediately at the first drum. The Romans are unfamiliar with the *bodhrán*. They won't know the sound."

Ailpein said, "Last time we killed at least three hundred. There are over seven thousand of them in this legion alone. How long do you think these attacks will work?"

"I don't know," replied Calach. "We shall see. We'll take small bites, and change tactics as necessary. The point is to keep them off guard, and not let them engage us to their advantage, using their tactics in open battle."

The second attack came off as planned, without a hitch. Over four hundred Picts stole into the camp through the gates that had been opened by the scouts, who had noiselessly overcome the doubled midnight guard. Each Pict took out two men as planned, but this time they used knives to slit the Romans' throats in their sleep, or in the rude awakening to the blade.

There was no scream, and no call to alarm. The subtle, almost imperceptible beating of the *bodhráns* began, and the Picts slipped back out of the camp into the night. The pipes began their ghostly drone, drawing sword-bearing Romans from their tents, primed for battle. The Romans found no one there to fight, and at first took that to mean it was a false alarm. Perhaps the enemy was simply playing a cruel joke.

Then the screams began. Entire tents had been decimated, drenched in blood. In sardonic wit, some of the Picts had placed severed heads as gruesome sentries outside the openings of assaulted tents. They gaped in the frozen horror of their abrupt death as their compatriots fell into terrified chaos, looking wildly about the camp in a vain attempt to identify their elusive attackers.

Felix stood trembling in the night, holding his unused sword loosely at his side. In full armor, he felt utterly vulnerable to the phantoms that had struck his legion once again, unchallenged, with total impunity, and slaughtered over eight hundred well-armed soldiers. His fear grew, shaking him to the core.

Quintus, Aquila, and several of the tribunes rushed to the center of the camp. Quintus bellowed in anger for order in the camp and for the centurions to report to him. Slowly, order returned. Quintus convened the centurions once again to assess this second raid, and to try to make sense of what had happened. It was clear to all of them that this was a strange and unprecedented enemy, with skill and guile such as they had never before encountered. Quintus knew that to engage in guerrilla warfare with these barbarians would be futile, but at the same time, these infuriating attacks would destroy the legion quickly if they were not stopped.

Quintus decided to quadruple the midnight guard, and to double the reinforcements of all future fortifications constructed in this god-forsaken land. If he could not draw the Picts into open battle, this would be a long, bloody, and maddening campaign.

15

Guerrilla War

CALACH AND HIS growing army staged two more midnight attacks on the Ninth Legion, each more devastating than the one before it. It wasn't until the last of the four attacks that the Picts took casualties, and the Romans finally saw the face of their daunting foe. The attack was almost finished when a Roman soldier awoke and sounded the alarm.

The Romans, frustrated by the repeated attacks, sprang into action with a vengeance. As fleeing Picts disappeared over the walls and through the open fortress gates, several dozen were forced to turn and fight the Romans who attacked them from behind. In the end, twenty-seven Picts lay dead, along with over five hundred Romans who had died in their beds, in the same manner that fourteen hundred of their fellow legionnaires had died in the previous three attacks.

When the last attack was over, curious soldiers gathered around the first Pictish warriors they had encountered since the march began. They wondered at the markings and tinting that covered their naked bodies, and the fact that they had gone into battle wearing nothing but their paint and heavy jewelry.

The Romans were impressed by the lean, powerful physique that appeared to be characteristic of these warriors. But what puzzled them most was that almost a third of them were women, all marked and dyed in the same manner as the men, and all equally naked. The women fought with swords, and exceptionally well. They had held their own against seasoned Roman swordsmen. None of those gathered had ever faced an enemy army that included women. The idea was foreign to them, and disconcerting.

Most significantly, the physical sight of the fierce and mysterious enemy that had until that moment eluded them while exacting a painful toll upon their ranks inspired awe and respect among the remaining Roman soldiers. The loss of so many of their own to this mere twenty-seven enemy dead was both remarkable and alarming to all of them.

In total, the four midnight attacks had reduced the Roman ranks by almost two thousand men, or nearly a sixth of its strength. Quintus sent well-armed messengers to the Twentieth Legion to advise Agricola of his dire situation, but the messengers never reached the Twentieth. They were simply swallowed up by this damned barbarian land.

It was almost two months before Agricola heard news from Quintus, and when he did it was a routine update. He heard nothing of the Ninth Legion's crippling losses. The Picts had intercepted messenger units that Quintus had dispatched to Agricola, and replaced them with Pretani men who donned the captured uniforms, posed as conscripts, and completed the messengers' missions. They reported to Agricola that all was well, and that there was nothing more to report.

Agricola, having met no resistance in what seemed to him to be an uninhabited land, was stunned. He was puzzled by the absence of an apparently elusive local population. There was no resistance to his obvious intention to conquer and claim this land. He did not realize that he was constantly surrounded by a considerable Pictish force that lurked just beyond his sight, and was allowing him to wander ever deeper into the belly of their ferocious beast.

Meanwhile, Calach and his army chipped away at the ruthless but terrified Ninth Legion. While Brude and the western contingent allowed the Twentieth to continue to drive deeper into the northwest, Calach focused the bulk of the Pictish forces against the Ninth Legion. The Picts had determined that not one soldier of the Ninth was to ever leave their land alive for what they had done to the village at Balloch.

Calach staged raids on marching columns, and smaller midnight attacks that were never as successful as the first few had been. For weeks before each midnight raid, Calach would have the pipers play throughout the night, on random nights. That practice threw the Romans off, so that they never knew whether the pipes announced a raid. When it didn't, the pipes kept the soldiers awake through a restless and eerie night. When it did, the attack took on a surreal, dreamlike quality.

To further the Romans' confusion, some raids were carried out in complete silence, and announced by the pipers at the break of dawn. The overall effect of the Picts' use of pipes and drums was a persistent and profound feeling of doom among the Roman soldiers.

The Romans of the Ninth Legion slowly began to adapt to the guerrilla warfare in which they had found themselves embroiled. They grew better able to defend themselves, but Quintus suspected that the annihilation of Balloch had sealed this legion's fate. He began to realize that while Agricola had probably overestimated the size of both the Pictish population and its armies, he had seriously underestimated their military prowess and their ability to unite. He had certainly not counted on an army that included female warriors who were just as fierce and capable as their male counterparts, and who could stand against the best Roman soldiers. That factor alone nearly doubled the effectiveness of the Pictish resistance forces.

The guerilla war dragged on through the rest of that year, and into the winter, with Roman losses far outpacing the Picts' casualties. By winter, the Ninth Legion had been reduced to a third of its original size.

The Roman army customarily spent winters rebuilding and fortifying their positions, and preparing for renewed battle in the spring. Constant harassment from the Picts made that difficult for the Ninth Legion this winter, and it wore upon their nerves.

Calach decided to let the Ninth Legion languish through the winter, hemmed in and harassed from all sides. The Picts continued to intercept Quintus's messenger units and replace them with the Pretani substitutes. The Pretani "messengers" delivered optimistic updates to Agricola, who became convinced that the Ninth was making easy progress after having overcome some initial Pictish resistance. Agricola was looking forward to a triumphant reunion of the two legions, and the pronouncement of the total subjugation of the Britannic Island.

Toward the end of winter, Calach called a council to plan a final, massive raid on the Ninth Legion before spring arrived and the Romans grew more prepared for battle. He sent word to Brude that the victorious eastern contingent would join his western forces in early spring to begin the war against Agricola's Twentieth.

Calach proposed a break from the tactics he had employed successfully until now. He was growing impatient with the grinding fatigue of this constant state of war, and he was anxious to end it and return to the normalcy of the life he had built with Fiona.

Most of Calach's captains disagreed. Most notable among them was Gabhran, who rarely contradicted Calach in public, but who had the firm support of Calach's closest advisors.

"We have built sufficient numbers and strength to overpower these Romans," Calach declared. "They will not withstand our force."

Fiona and Gabhran had arrived with another massive group of recruits, and the total unified Pictish army had grown to nearly twelve thousand strong. There were four thousand warriors under Brude's command, shadowing the Twentieth Legion in the west, and over eight thousand surrounding the besieged Ninth under Calach. Calach's force had nearly doubled throughout the winter, as warriors continued to arrive to join the fight.

Ailpein cleared his throat, and Calach cast him an expectant look.

"The Romans are built and trained for head on conflict. They are comfortable in the field, and adept at maneuvering in the open. Our strength has been in denying them that latitude."

Gabhran nodded in agreement.

"We can easily overwhelm them," Calach insisted. "They are tired and worn, and far from home. We have denied them most of their supply lines throughout the winter. I believe they are ready to go home. I believe we can crush them."

"Why crush them?" Domhnall asked. "A hunter can rush a wild boar and overpower it with the force of his arms, at the risk of serious injury, and thank the gods for a successful hunt at the end of the day. Or he can hunt in the Pictish way, laying traps and inflicting a hundred wounds, each weakening the boar until it collapses from the steady loss of blood. He'll still go home – uninjured – and thank the gods for a successful hunt. What advantage has he to hurry the hunt and risk injury?"

"I want this over," Calach said, simply.

"At what price?" asked Ailpein.

"If we can rush them, root them out, and utterly defeat them within their own gates, where they cannot maneuver," he said, pausing to look hard at Ailpein, "then we can all go home victorious to our wives and children and our peaceful life. Enough of this damned war. I want to get it over with."

"Your impatience is getting the best of you," Gabhran gently warned.

Somewhere in the back of Calach's mind, Gabhran's warning resonated with words he had heard long ago, on his private craggy ridge.

"We are not pressed for time," Gabhran continued softly. "We have all the time in the world. We have lived here for a thousand years, and we will live here for a thousand more. We should stay with the tactics that have worked for us until they are driven away."

"They'll be overwhelmed within the walls of their fort," Calach pressed. "They will not be permitted to maneuver. We'll appear in the night, surprise them at dawn, and slaughter them as they try to wipe the sleep from their fearful eyes. The pipes will wail and the drums will beat, and by the time the sun reaches its peak nothing will remain but blood and dust and rotting flesh. We will take to the road with the sounds of happy buzzards echoing behind us."

Calach's captains remained unconvinced and sat shaking their heads in disagreement. Only one captain, Dungal, a Smertae who had been closely allied with Brude, showed any interest in Calach's plan. Ailpein cast a suspicious eye toward Dungal. Calach caught the look, and he focused his attention on the Smertae.

"What say you, Dungal?" Calach asked. "You've been quiet."

Dungal stood and looked warily at the other captains, who looked equally warily back at him. Domhnall's eyes narrowed as he waited to hear Dungal's words. He clearly suspected that Dungal would be speaking for Brude.

"Calach's plan will work," Dungal said. "It's a change in tactics that the Romans won't expect."

Calach nodded, but he noted the suspicion in his good friend Ailpein's eyes. He trusted Ailpein, and he knew he should lean toward his advice over Dungal's approval. But Calach felt too strongly about the issue, and he opted instead to accept Dungal's approval as validation of his plan.

"Calach has led us well so far," Dungal said. Ailpein shook his head in barely concealed disgust. "There's no reason to doubt him now. I say we launch an all out attack on the fort, as Calach suggests. I would guess that Brude would agree with me."

Calach stopped at the mention of Brude's name. He thought it odd, and misplaced in this gathering. He looked around the semi-circle of his captains, sensing the division and the consternation among them. Against his better judgment, he pronounced his decision on the manner of the next attack.

This was to be the Picts first all out assault on the Romans since the Romans had crossed the Tweed.

Calach and the captains formulated the plan to attack the Ninth Legion from all sides, slipping noiselessly and en masse inside the fort, and then with the sudden fanfare of the pipes and drums, launch the attack.

Inside the fort, in close combat, denied their most effective battle tactics, the Romans would be on equal footing with the Picts. Calach knew that the Romans were both weakened and disheartened, and that that would diminish their strength.

But Calach also knew instinctively that this would be the first time the Romans were cornered and outnumbered. They would truly be fighting for their lives.

"Be wary, men," Calach warned. "We go this time to fight a cornered boar, which will fight for its life with nothing left to lose. Do not assume that our victory is certain. Fight with the desperation of dying men!"

The attack began before dawn on a frigid winter day, to the sudden cacophony of the Pictish pipes and drums. Calach stood just outside the

gates with Fiona and Gabhran and a thousand other warriors behind
him. There were another two thousand positioned in a ring around the
fort, just inside the tree line, waiting for any Romans that might escape
the attack. The rest of the Picts had poured over the walls of the fort.

Calach heard the first cries and the clash of battle ringing from
within as he waited for his men to throw the gates open.

The Romans did indeed fight with the strength of desperate men.
They understood their grim predicament, and they were determined to
fight to the last breath. It took a moment longer than Calach had
anticipated for his men to open the gate. He glanced at Gabhran with a
look of concern just as the gates finally flew open.

Uvin, one of Calach's cousins, had thrown it wide, and he now stood
with both fists raised, screaming a triumphant war cry. As Calach
strode forward to embrace his cousin, a Roman spear impaled Uvin
from behind, pinning him to the ground at Calach's feet. Calach turned
and screamed to the Picts at the gate to attack without mercy. They
eagerly complied, and a tidal wave of screaming Picts streamed into the
fort.

Calach spoke a quick word into Uvin's ear as he lay dying, and then
he sprang into battle.

Gabhran rushed forward to attack a fleeing Roman soldier, but
Calach caught Gabhran from behind. Calach pulled Gabhran's face
close to his own.

"Remember your mission!" Calach snarled, motioning toward
Fiona. "She is your only concern!" Gabhran nodded his assent, and
moved in close behind Fiona as she swung her sword at an advancing
Roman soldier. Calach turned to engage two Romans who were quickly
advancing on him.

The battle raged for a quarter of an hour. Calach noted that the
Picts were sustaining more casualties than he had thought they might,
and he could see that the Romans were indeed desperate for their lives.

Despite his warning, Calach could see that many of his warriors were overconfident after months of inflicting heavy losses upon the Romans.

Calach was considering how to regain their lost momentum when the pipes suddenly began to sound retreat from the surrounding hills. Calach stopped, bewildered, along with the rest of his warriors.

Who had called retreat?

In that momentary lull, the Romans sprang into a fury against the Picts.

Against his will, to avoid chaos, Calach forced himself to repeat the call for retreat. Confusion spread among the Picts. Calach looked about for Gabhran and Fiona, but he could see them nowhere.

He repeated the call again, and most of the Picts responded to his second call. Some kept fighting, either in stubbornness or because they were not in a position to disengage. The furious Romans gained ground as most of the Picts retreated through the gates.

Calach grew increasingly alarmed. He still could not locate Fiona. He began to run wildly around the fort, swinging his sword when necessary, but focusing on his search for her. He cursed the retreat and wondered why it had been sounded.

Calach did not know that Agricola had sent two cohorts from the Twentieth Legion on a routine visit to the Ninth, or that they had unexpectedly engaged the Picts surrounding the fort.

As Calach frantically searched the fort, he finally caught sight of Fiona. She was squared off against a Roman swordsman, and another was coming at her from behind. For a brief moment he oddly thought how beautiful she was, her hair laced tightly, and her eyes blazing fury. He looked for Gabhran, who suddenly appeared between Fiona and the approaching Roman, whom he engaged. Calach moved toward them to ensure that they could join the retreat.

As Calach fought his way toward Fiona and Gabhran, he tried to keep his eyes fixed upon them. He was perhaps thirty feet away when she saw him. She hesitated briefly at the sight of him, and then returned her attention to her foe. Calach dispatched a Roman who had swung his sword in an arc toward his head, and he turned for a final sprint to Fiona's side.

Fiona and her opponent were nearly evenly matched, but Fiona's persistence and agility was beginning to wear the Roman down. He was moving backward under each blow of Fiona's sword, and his eyes shifted seeking a firmer position than the one into which she was maneuvering him.

Fiona glanced once more in Calach's direction for reassurance of his safety. Her eyes lingered for a brief moment, just long enough for the Roman to catch her glance. He followed her eyes toward Calach. The Roman was momentarily startled by the imposing sight of Calach thundering toward him, but he caught himself and returned his attention to Fiona.

Calach shook his head quickly at Fiona, and he nodded urgently toward her opponent to direct her attention where it belonged. Fiona complied, and she whirled, swinging her sword at blinding speed down upon the crouching Roman. Fiona's sword cut through the Roman's armor, and down through the shoulder beneath it, severing his arm and continuing into his chest. The Roman shuddered under the blow, his face a mask of horror.

In the same instant, a centurion freed himself from grappling with a Pict, and he swung around to face Fiona and her foe. In a burst of rage, he swung his sword in a brutal arc toward Fiona's side. Calach watched in slow motion as the sword cut deep into her side, knocking her off balance as she pulled her own sword from her fallen foe's chest.

Fiona fell to her knees under the centurion's blow. Blood flowed from the deep gash in her side. Calach screamed in desperate rage. He lunged forward as the centurion raised his sword to strike again.

Calach watched in horror, running as if through mud, as the Roman raised his bloody sword skyward. Fiona pushed herself to her knees, and again her eyes sought Calach. Their eyes locked as Calach strained to reach her, and the Roman brought his sword down with brutal force.

Calach did not reach Fiona in time. The sword passed through her neck, and it rang loudly as it struck the solid ground.

Calach felt as though he had been struck with the force of a thousand blows. Agony pierced his heart as the reality of what he had seen registered in his screaming mind.

The centurion who had killed Fiona turned toward Calach, leering. Calach swung forcefully as he came upon the centurion. He brought his sword down hard, slicing easily through the centurion's gleaming helmet, through the top of his head, and continuing deep into the center of his neck. The halves of the centurion's helmet skittered wildly in opposite directions, and the sound of it echoed oddly in Calach's ears.

Calach and the dead centurion sank slowly to their knees. Calach's face was frozen in a silent, agonized scream.

Gabhran turned to face the gut wrenching sight. He tore himself out of his momentary shock and lunged forward, pushing Calach out of the path of two descending Romans. Gabhran turned to engage them, and he was joined by two more Picts who had come to Calach's aid. They quickly killed the two Romans, and then stood guard as Gabhran lifted Calach to his feet and began to guide him toward the gate.

Calach could have absorbed almost anything but what he had just witnessed. His pleas for Fiona to stay out of this battle screamed mercilessly through the chaos of his reeling mind. Her defiant look still shimmered before his eyes. The defiance in those eyes suddenly transformed into a look of deepest sorrow, and then into the vacant stare that looked upon him now from the dusty ground.

Calach could not move. He suddenly did not care if he lived or died. He was vaguely aware of Romans straining to reach him, their swords singing through the air as they descended upon him, only to be cut down by the Picts that ringed their stricken leader.

The cries of his captains urged Calach to turn away from the sight, to turn back to the fight. Beyond their pleading, Calach heard a faint and whispering voice calling him to strength, and urging him to find the will to live. It was an old and familiar voice from long ago, and it somehow filled him with inhuman strength and resolve.

Finally, at the urging of the voice and the cries around him, Calach summoned the strength to tear himself from his stupor. He was vaguely aware of the imperative that he should pull himself together if the Picts were to survive this battle, which had suddenly gone very terribly wrong.

Calach vehemently cursed his decision to launch such a risky attack upon the Roman fort. As the weight of the consequences of that decision pressed upon him, he also began to curse his own life as well.

16

Decimation of the Ninth

THE PICTS LOST ALMOST two thousand warriors in the disastrous attack on the Ninth Legion fort. In spite of his personal devastation, Calach had led them as they fought their way through the new arrivals from the Twentieth Legion, while defending themselves from the Ninth Legion soldiers who harried them from the rear.

The Picts retreated well beyond their forward camp, hoping that the bulk of the Romans would stay at the fort to regroup, rather than pursue them.

Calach was stung by this bitter setback, but his personal tragedy made the sting of defeat feel numb in comparison. Fiona was the love of his life. She was everything to him, and the only future for which he had ever hoped.

His mood swung wildly between boiling rage and hopeless despair, and sometimes it seemed to be a swirling mix of the two. He struggled with every fiber of his being to withstand the excruciating pain, and to focus on the war. Gabhran did his best to console Calach, but for the most part he failed.

Weeks dragged by as Calach mourned. He fell deeper into dark brooding, mostly retreating to the thin solace of his tent, while Gabhran put his energies into keeping the Picts motivated to finish the fight whenever the opportunity arose.

Rumors began to surface that Calach was no longer willing or able to lead the stalled army. Gabhran struggled in vain to counter the dampening effects of growing doubts.

Finally, on a crisp, clear morning toward the end of the third idle week, Calach emerged from his tent. He stood tall on unsteady feet, his swollen eyes blazing hatred and pain. Gabhran rushed to him, and Calach glared hard into his eyes. In a guttural growl that Gabhran could hardly believe came from his brother, Calach vowed that they would destroy every last Roman in the land. He ordered Gabhran to rally the troops and prepare for a final, brutal attack upon the remaining Romans.

The Picts pulled together, thankful to be on the move again at last. In the lull, they had licked their wounds and subdued the trepidation that had come of their defeat.

Calach went into battle like a man possessed. There was hatred and fury, the likes of which none had ever seen in him. In unsettled them, but they did the only thing they knew to do. They followed him into battle.

Calach himself was the first to breach the wall. The Romans at the gate were stunned at the frightening sight of him. If ever a Pict had resembled a demon from hell, this one did. The sentries literally fell to their knees in a futile attempt to surrender at his feet.

Calach would have none of that this day. His furious sword moved more swiftly than any they had ever seen, and the sentries' heads fell quickly, one by one. They all died before the first body hit the ground.

Even the Picts who accompanied Calach kept a distance from his frenzied rage. They stood in awe, having no one left at the gate for them to fight.

The alarm went up. Surprised Romans rushed toward the invading Picts. Calach threw the gate open to a tidal wave of Picts that flooded into the fort. The Picts fought with a vengeance, and it was clear from the start that the Romans in the fort were doomed.

After raging intensely for almost an hour, the battle finally began to subside. Picts searched in vain for opponents, but found none. Those that could escape had done so. Those that remained were fighting in vain for their lives. Crowds of Picts gathered as spectators to the last remaining fights, and began to cheer for their champion in each of them. The Roman participants were deflated by the futility of their plight, and one by one they died.

Calach rushed to the central command tent. He had not seen Quintus or Aquila in the fight. When he got to the tent, he found it surrounded by centurions, all kneeling in surrender with their sword points to the ground. Calach signaled to the Picts to round them up, and he stormed into the tent.

Quintus, Aquila, and several of the senior centurions sat ashen-faced around a wooden table at one end of the tent. Calach strode over to face them, his bloodied sword at his side.

"You didn't join the fight," Calach spat. "What kind of men are you? Cowards!" Calach seized Quintus's collar and dragged him roughly toward the opening of the tent. Quintus's feet dragged helplessly as he struggled to gain his footing. Calach dragged him outside, while Ailpein dragged Aquila behind him. The other Picts took hold of the rest of the Romans and led them outside as well.

The Roman commanders stood blinking, blinded by the sun and astonished at the sight of thousands of their soldiers dead. The soldiers of the tent guard detail were being slaughtered without mercy a short distance away.

The commanders themselves were surrounded by the most frightening people any of them had ever seen. The Picts stood glowering at them, with wild hair and painted skin, their bodies covered with pictures of their demons and beasts, and with the blood of the soldiers who lie scattered about the camp. Quintus knew that their defeat had been utter and complete, and that he would soon die.

In that moment, Calach spied his brother not a hundred yards away. His heart sank. Gabhran lay face down in the dust, with blood flowing freely from his side. Calach screamed involuntarily as he sprang toward Gabhran.

Calach knelt beside his brother, and realized with a rush of relief that he was still alive. But Gabhran was wounded badly, and Calach was certain he would die. He could not bear this second devastating blow, and in that moment something broke inside his mind. He slumped, wracked by the most profound grief.

Quintus looked upon Calach and tried to imagine his emotions. He began to wonder to himself why he was here, leading this army into a strange land to do nothing more than rob these people of all they had ever known. He began to glimpse the emptiness in what he had done. And then he flinched as Calach suddenly rose and turned to look at him.

Calach walked slowly toward the last Romans, as a lion stalks its ill-fated prey. His furious eyes bored into Quintus as he approached. Quintus thought that no man could ever look fiercer, and he prayed to his gods that his death would come quickly. He prayed in vain.

Calach stopped in front of the anxious Romans. A few of them began to shake visibly beneath his glare. Quintus looked warily at Calach, transfixed by his raging eyes.

Calach glared directly into Quintus's eyes as he walked slowly to the first quaking centurion. He removed a long blade from his belt and pressed it into the man's belly. With a grunt, he pushed the blade in and drew it upwards with steady force. The man let out a blood-curdling scream as his blood gushed to the ground. Calach held him there until he was dead, and then he angrily pushed the lifeless body from him. Without taking his eyes off of Quintus, he moved to the second, and then the third, savoring with each death the vengeance that was boiling in his heart.

He finally arrived in front of Aquila, the prefect, and shifted his gaze from Quintus to look into his eyes. He growled in the Pictish tongue, and a Pretani who stood behind Calach began to translate:

"I could cut your throat a thousand times and it would not be enough." Calach wrapped the fingers of his left hand around Aquila's throat and squeezed. "This death is too good for you, Roman pig." He placed the tip of his blade beneath Aquila's chin. "Die, and spend your eternity in torment!" He pushed the blade upward into Aquila's skull. When Aquila's convulsions finally ceased, Calach let him drop to the blood-drenched ground.

Finally, Calach stood facing Quintus. Tears streamed down Quintus's face. Quintus began to stammer, and the Pretani translated for Calach.

"Forgive me," he begged. "I wish that none of this had ever been."

Calach's lips curled into an ugly grimace. He grasped Quintus's collar and pulled his face close. "In a moment you can carry that message to my *wife*," he growled. Again the Pretani translated.

Calach stepped backward, away from Quintus. He placed his right hand on the pommel of his sword, and continued to growl at Quintus.

"You came here to take what was never yours. You came to take our freedom and our land. But you have taken from me something far more precious to me than those. You have taken the life of my wife, and now, it would seem, my brother." Quintus's tears continued as he listened to the Pretani's translation.

"I am going to kill you now. But that will not be enough. If I see you in the next life, I will kill you then, too. For all of eternity, whenever our paths should cross, I swear to make you pay for what you have done to us here. You will never forget the horror you have brought to my people, or the grief that you have brought to me. I can only pray that your wife and your children will one day hear the details of how you died, and that they will live with that knowledge for the rest of their days."

Calach drew his sword and struck off Quintus's head.

17

Calach and Brude

DOMHNALL ORGANIZED a detail to carry Gabhran, struggling for his life, home to the Caledonii tribe along with dozens of other badly wounded warriors. After a long and emotional farewell, Calach kissed Gabhran's cheek and finally released his grip on Gabhran's hand. Calach watched in silence as they bore his brother on a stretcher to the chariot that would carry him home.

The rest of the Picts set out to join Brude's contingent in the west.

Several days later, the gate sentry at the Twentieth Legion fort sounded an announcement of arrivals at the gate. Agricola, along with his Prefect and a dozen centurions, peered through the gate as it opened, curious at what they saw.

Two centuriae of Pretani conscripts from the Ninth Legion stood in formation waiting for the Governor to address them. Agricola strode to stand in front of them, and commanded them to report. The Pretani captain stepped forward and saluted.

"Your delegation to the Ninth Legion returns, My Lord. And with them, the great and victorious Ninth Legion arrives as well, having vanquished their enemy completely."

The Pretani soldier saluted smartly and stepped back into formation. Agricola craned his neck to see the accompanying army behind them, to no avail. The Pretani captain barked an order, and the detail turned and marched forty paces to the left, revealing a row of horse-drawn wagons facing rearward toward the fort.

"Your leave, My Lord," the Pretani begged, mocking the general with a smirk. The Pretani executed a perfect about-face, and then marched double time toward the trees.

A dozen Picts in Roman uniforms tipped the wagons back, pouring thousands of empty, bloodied Roman helmets to the ground. Riders spurred the horses, emptying the carts, into which the rest of the Picts sprang to make their escape.

Agricola watched in dismay at the brazen display, and at the sheer number of battered helmets rolling awkwardly down the hill toward his feet.

Beyond the mounds of helmets, Agricola saw a lone Roman spear stuck fast into the ground. At the top of the spear, Agricola recognized the face his long time friend and compatriot. The searching eyes and gaping mouth of Quintus's severed head nearly mirrored the shocked expression on Agricola's face.

Maniacal laughter rang through the trees as the Picts and the Pretani disappeared into the darkness beyond them. Agricola swore angrily and stormed back toward the fort.

Calach had just arrived at Brude's camp with his battle-worn contingent from the east. Brude was dismayed by Calach's appearance. He seemed a different person from the one to whom he had bid farewell almost a year earlier.

Brude threw his arms around his battered general, hugging him with apparent warmth. He stepped back and looked around at Calach's captains, and then he turned back to Calach with a questioning look.

"Where is your brother?" Brude asked.

Calach's face darkened and he turned away, his shoulders slumping. His matted hair hid his face, and his hands were tightly clenched, his knuckles white.

"Fiona's dead," Ailpein answered quietly, trying to shield the words from Calach. "Gabhran is bad off, gone home to Muthill to fight for his life."

The news shocked Brude. He shot a look of dismay toward Calach.

"How is he?" Brude asked, nodding in Calach's direction. Ailpein shook his head sadly and said nothing. The journey west had been difficult for everyone. Calach's brooding silence, interspersed with sporadic bouts of fury, had cast a pall over the Picts, and chilled the enthusiasm of their victory. To Ailpein, it had felt much like a funeral march.

"The loss has hit him hard, as it would anyone," Ailpein said. "I can not begrudge him his fury. He's very strong, of course, but his healing will take much time. The sooner we finish this, the better. We've all suffered, and want to go home."

"Can he lead?" Brude asked. He was evaluating Calach now. Ailpein suspected he might be plotting a bit, as well.

"He can lead. Nothing will distract him from this war." Ailpein stared hard at Brude, and added, "You need not concern yourself with that."

"Is that right? Need I not?" Brude turned on Ailpein. "Wouldn't that be exactly what I should be doing right now? I have my men to think about, and the danger if you are wrong."

"He said that I am fine!" Calach roared. Calach had heard every word, and Brude turned now to face Calach's fierce glare. "Come away

from Ailpein now, and face me. What have you to say to me?" Calach
demanded.

Brude hesitated.

"I...I need to know if you are fit to lead," Brude stammered. "You
are...injured. You don't seem well," Brude said. After a pause,
"Perhaps it would be prudent for me to relieve–"

"Enough!" Calach snapped. "Don't say the words." Calach sensed
Brude's motive, and would not have it. "I lead this army. Unless you
are prepared to kill me, you will not challenge me again." Calach
squared off in front of Brude, so that their faces were inches apart. "Did
you think that you might relieve me of command?"

"If it's necessary, it should be so. It might be best for this army,"
Brude said. "You've suffered much. Your judgment may not be–"

"I said enough," Calach repeated, interrupting him. "I'll not say it
again. If you have trouble with my leading of this army, then you
should leave now for home. I well know that your concern is not for this
army, but for yourself. I will not allow your ambition to fracture this
army, regardless of my condition."

Brude spat on the ground at Calach's feet. He squared his
shoulders, and placed his hand on the hilt of his dagger.

"And I," Brude hissed, "will not allow your poor judgment to
endanger the rest of us."

A crowd began to gather. Ailpein stood ready to defend Calach if
necessary. He stepped forward and placed a hand on Brude's chest.
Brude grasped the hand and twisted it sharply as he swung around to
confront Ailpein. The clatter of swords pulled sharply from their
sheaths filled the air.

"Enough!" Calach bellowed. The unearthly sound froze Brude
where he stood, and silence fell over the camp. Brude had never seen
Calach so angry, or heard him quite so loud, like thunder cracking
through the rising din. He began to realize that Calach was no longer
the man he had known.

Brude turned back to face Calach, whose eyes bore deeply into his own. Brude could almost feel their fire on his skin. Calach spoke as a man possessed, his voice growling low and guttural.

"I will have no more of your scheming," Calach snapped. "I will have no more of your jealousy. I will have nothing but your complete and utter loyalty and support. If you do not have it in you to give, then leave or I will kill you. It is your choice. Make it now. There will be no more of this."

The two men faced one another in silence for what seemed an endless moment. The tension in the camp was palpable. No spectator dared to break the silence.

Brude's resentment of Calach began to ebb, making way for grudging respect and a new and insidious fear. There was only one thing he could do to end this standoff in his favor, and to his surprise he had already begun to do it. Brude removed his right hand from his dagger and extended it toward Calach with his palm turned up.

Calach stared into Brude's eyes for a long moment. His face softened slightly, and then he gruffly grasped Brude's shaking, outstretched hand. He pulled Brude close and threw his left arm around his brawny shoulders. As he held Brude tightly, with his mouth close to Brude's ear, Calach spoke softly, almost imperceptibly.

"If you ever do that again," Calach whispered, "by the gods I will kill you where you stand."

Brude stiffened. He well knew the magnitude of his mistake.

18

Brude's Scheme

AILPEIN RUSHED EXCITEDLY into Calach's tent, with Domhnall running breathlessly close behind. Calach had been brooding in silence since daybreak, in the darkness of his tent. Ailpein strained to see him in the shadows.

Calach had been wrestling with his torment, trying to overcome the bitterness and anger that had consumed him. He was painfully aware that he had succumbed to the very things that his father, and Girom, and his own heart had always warned him to avoid. At this moment he was weighted down by the magnitude of his failure. He was struggling to recover from the fall.

"Calach!" Ailpein cried. "Domhnall has returned from Muthill." Calach sprang up at that, anxious for word of Gabhran and the other wounded warriors. Domhnall threw his arms eagerly around his friend and hugged him tightly.

"My brother…it's good to see you. I have great news. Gabhran lives. He is well, and he is improving every day. He'll regain his strength in time."

Calach collapsed into a chair and raised his eyes toward the sky, breathing a deep sigh of relief. Thankful tears welled in his eyes.

"Thank you, my friend," Calach said. "That's the best news I've heard in many weeks. And the others?"

"Many died on the way home," Domhnall said mournfully. "Those who lived are well enough. Most of them wish they could have returned with us to fight again." Domhnall relayed all the news from home while Calach and Ailpein listened quietly.

The entire tribe was in deep mourning for Fiona, he said. She was widely regarded as a princess of the tribe, even though Calach would never have accepted a crown. Her loss had shaken the Caledonii, as had their heartfelt worry for Calach's welfare.

"They can't wait to see you home again, Calach," Domhnall said.

"Nor can I," said Calach, his voice barely a whisper.

Ailpein told Domhnall of Calach's confrontation with Brude. Domhnall grew angry, and he swore to do terrible things to Brude, should anything like it happen again. Calach waved his hand, assuring them both that he had put Brude firmly into his place, and that there would be no repeat. Ailpein's face revealed his doubts, and Domhnall shook his head.

"Don't trust him," Domhnall said.

"I don't," replied Calach. "I never did. But we can't afford a split in this army. For all of his faults, many do respect him. One day he could be chosen king of the Smertae. If that happens, I would rather have him as an ally than an enemy."

The Smertae were a small tribe, but Calach still preferred that they did not become enemies of the Caledonii. The Roman threat had convinced Calach more than ever that the tribes must maintain their new federation in some tangible form. He would not allow petty conflicts to hinder that. He would somehow have to make a lasting peace with Brude.

"I must ask you, Calach," Domhnall finally said. "How is your heart, really? Are you going to be all right?"

Calach looked long into Domhnall's worried eyes.

"Yes. I will survive this," Calach assured him. "My heart is bleeding, and I want to destroy the world in my rage. My pain is tearing me apart. But I must see that we finish this fight. We must drive these heartless bastards from our lands."

Calach's determination reassured his anxious friends.

Ailpein forced a laugh to try to lighten the mood. "You've had us worried, you have," he said. He gave Calach's shoulder a warm squeeze. "We're with you, brother, until the end. I'm glad you'll be all right."

The three men talked long into the night, planning and debating how best to deal with the remaining Roman legion. Brude glanced toward the tent occasionally, glowering from his seat by a flickering fire. He was flooded with chaotic thoughts and emotions that competed for control of his intentions. Brude was a troubled man.

Another brooding man with a gloomy face sat close by Brude, watching him intently through squinted eyes. Bhaltair was a lowly man of little means, and he was of Brude's Smertae clan. Bhaltair had known Brude his entire life, and yet Brude knew Bhaltair not at all. Bhaltair had never really liked Brude, but then he had never really liked anyone else, either.

Bhaltair sidled closer toward Brude, and he rubbed his hands vigorously by the fire.

Brude turned to Bhaltair in annoyance. Bhaltair returned a solemn grin.

"What do you want?" Brude demanded.

"What, indeed," Bhaltair replied, nodding toward Calach's tent. "What do you make of him, the would-be king?" Brude stared stoically at the man, and then he slowly shifted his gaze to the depths of the blazing fire. Bhaltair prodded.

"He'll be our death," Bhaltair continued. "That much is certain. He's unyielding…stubborn. Maybe too stubborn to see the benefits of another way."

"What do you mean?" growled Brude. "What benefits? What other way?"

Bhaltair glanced nervously around them, checking to be sure that no one else was in earshot.

"You've seen the Roman soldiers, have you not?" Bhaltair asked. "They're not all Roman, you know. And yet even the non-Romans are well-fed…well-clothed. Even paid, most of them."

"Speak plainly," Brude commanded. "Be clear, or I'll see that you lose your tongue."

Bhaltair swallowed hard and looked around again. He leaned closer to Brude, and spoke barely above a whisper. He knew that he was taking a terrible risk, but he was certain that he had read Brude well.

"What are we fighting against," Bhaltair hissed, "but an army that would welcome us as brothers if we would only let them. They don't want to kill us! No! They only want us to be Roman. Is that so very bad? To be called a Roman?"

Brude's eyes widened at Bhaltair's words.

"Quiet!" Brude growled hotly. "Not another word. Never… *never* repeat those words to anyone, not to any other soul. Swear it!"

"I…I…swear it," Bhaltair squeaked. He had obviously misread Brude, and he was certain that he would very soon regret it.

"It is treason," Brude barked. He stood to confront the diminutive man, who was suddenly trembling and wishing he could disappear. Brude turned and strode away into the night. Bhaltair shrunk away slowly in the opposite direction, seeking his own sanctuary from the scrutiny of the firelight.

The next day Calach called a meeting of the tribal chiefs. He made a point of calling Brude to sit by his side, and requesting his insight into the strategies and tactics under review. His efforts to bring Brude into his circle, to make peace with his rival, reassured the Picts, and the mood grew lighter as the day wore on.

But later that evening Ailpein noticed that Brude had gone. He had taken to noting Brude's whereabouts and actions throughout each day, as a matter of discretion. And now Brude was nowhere to be found. Ailpein gathered a handful of scouts to find him, and then to report back.

At that very moment Bhaltair was cursing his miscalculation as Brude dragged him roughly by the collar toward a pair of waiting horses.

"Congratulations, my wee genius! You're now my new lieutenant. And you'll accompany me on the most important mission in the land. We're off to change our world for the better, you and me."

It did not take long for Ailpein's men to track Brude and his reluctant lieutenant as they made their way toward the fort that served as the headquarters of Agricola's Twentieth Legion.

It was several days' ride over rough terrain, but Brude traveled with the speed of a man possessed. It appeared to Ailpein's scouts that Brude's pace had pushed the frail lieutenant's body close to death, but Brude betrayed little concern for that minor annoyance. They arrived at Agricola's fort late on the third hard day.

Brude hailed the gate guard loudly, and was admitted without delay.

It was not long before Brude stood awkwardly in front of the Roman general, who sat comfortably behind a heavy oak table in the center of his command quarters. The table had been hewn by hand from a mighty oak in Lower Britannia by the best of Pretani craftsmen. Agricola thought it fitting that his battle plans were routinely laid upon the finest of his enemy's wood crafted by his enemy's finest hands. Agricola looked up at the odious Pict who had come to him uninvited and unwelcome.

Brude rushed forward to grasp the general's hand, thinking that it would be proper to kiss his ring, or something equally gracious.

Agricola's hands remained firmly in his lap. Brude stood awkwardly for a moment while Bhaltair sniggered quietly behind him. Brude glared at Bhaltair as he moved back to a respectable distance from the table.

"What do you want from me?" Agricola demanded curtly. Brude stiffened at Agricola's unexpected gruffness, while a Pretani guard translated his words.

"The same thing that you may want, perhaps," Brude ventured. Bhaltair stared blankly at the back of Brude's head. Agricola's face twisted in disbelief, and he looked at Brude with contempt.

"You're my enemy. I want you dead." Agricola said the words slowly, calmly, to make sure that there was no mistake about their truth.

Brude swayed backward almost imperceptibly, and he trembled involuntarily. He snorted in surprise, while Bhaltair sniggered again, more nervously this time. Bhaltair had anticipated that things might take this course. Brude quickly regained his composure.

"I need not be your enemy," Brude continued. Agricola raised his eyebrows.

"You're offering me your services as a spy?" While Agricola understood the value of his network of spies, he knew them all to be selfish, fickle men, unworthy of his esteem.

Brude shook his head violently.

"A spy? No! Not a spy..."

"What then? What do you want?"

"I want peace."

"You want peace," Agricola repeated, laughing. "We all want peace," he said, glancing mirthfully at his commanders' stony faces. Each had his hand upon his sword. Agricola looked back at Brude. "And your death would bring us all peace." His words hung in the air.

"Perhaps there's another way," Brude finally said.

Agricola sat wordlessly, gazing at Brude. He shifted in his seat to look at Bhaltair. He sniffed at the sight of the little man, and then returned his attention to Brude.

"Enlighten me," Agricola snapped.

Brude breathed deeply, and he carefully crafted his words.

"We are facing a long and bloody war," Brude began. "Many of the casualties will be yours. Even if you succeed, what is left of your army will bear witness to the difficulties you endured against our people. The brilliance of your victory will be dulled by the damage you will sustain in the process."

"Go on," Agricola allowed. "I assume you have a proposal."

"I do. I have a proposal that should be profitable for the both of us, as well as for our people. I propose to end this war."

The room fell silent. Bhaltair's eyes grew wide in uneasy anticipation. He had not been apprised of the details or the extent of Brude's plan. Agricola was clearly shocked and intrigued.

"What authority do you have to end this war?" Agricola challenged. Brude ignored the question.

"My men are tired of this war. Many wish only to go home to their families and their farms."

"And how do you propose to end it?"

Brude swallowed hard.

"Suppose the Picts were to submit to Roman rule," he said, "to agree to become a part of your empire, without a fight."

Agricola said nothing. He fixed his gaze on Brude as he considered the weight of Brude's words. He suspected a ruse, but he knew that one such as this was unlikely to have originated in the depths of this brute's mind. *No*, he thought, *he is here on Calach's behalf, to trick me.*

"Capitulation? Why would the Picts capitulate?" Agricola asked. "What could you possibly do to bring this to pass?"

"As I've said, many are tired of this war. Many wish only to go home. And some," he paused to make his meaning clear, "long for the advantages that would come with Roman citizenship."

To Agricola, Brude's meaning was all too embarrassingly clear.

"You are of the Smertae, are you not?" Agricola asked. Brude was surprised by Agricola's awareness of that fact. "The Smertae are less than influential among the Picts. Yet you believe that you can sway not only your tribe, but the rest of the Picts as well?" The insult stung, but Brude could not allow is to distract him.

"I am well respected among all Picts," Brude insisted. "I enjoy high regard for noble deeds, and I am considered to be among the fiercest of our warriors. Besides, every Pict speaks for all Picts equally. My authority is as great as any other. There is nothing to prevent me from making this proposal to you, or from pressing it among my people."

"And Galgacus?" Agricola asked, his eyes piercing Brude's.

"Galgacus?" Brude did not know the name.

A Pretani dressed in the uniform of a centurion stepped toward Brude.

"Calach," he whispered. He nodded curtly toward Agricola, and added in a conspiratorial tone, "It's what they call him because they can't pronounce his name." The Pretani stepped back into his place with an amused grin.

"Galgacus," Agricola repeated, "your 'swordsman'. What of him?"

Brude cursed softly to himself. He had hoped that Calach would be of no consideration. He had planned to deal with Calach quietly, in the shadows. But now this Roman general had brought him into the matter.

"He will not give in," Brude declared. "He will not agree. He is an unreasonable man, and he will fight until we are all dead."

"Then it is his word I shall need, and not yours. Bring him to me, along with his word, and you shall have your wish."

"And what, exactly," Brude ventured, "shall I have?"

Agricola sighed impatiently.

"You are premature. But I give you this word: *if* the Picts capitulate, with absolutely no hostilities, then you shall have your freedom. You will be a citizen of Rome."

"A citizen? Nothing more?"

"What more would you like?" Agricola asked, perturbed.

"Office. A governorship, perhaps. Some reward for bringing peace."

"You want to rule your people," Agricola said, smirking.

"Reporting to you, of course," Brude nodded.

"Of course. Why not? A governorship. Bring me Galgacus, and you shall have your governorship."

"And my people?" Brude pressed.

"That depends on them," Agricola answered. "They'll be citizens, or servants, or slaves. Some may die. But those who wish peace shall have it, on Roman terms. Peace and safety and citizenship, and nothing more. They will be free to live, with the rights and the responsibilities of Romans."

"And 'Galgacus'?" Brude looked keenly into Agricola's eyes, willing him to say the words he longed to hear. After a momentary silence, he had the answer he sought.

"Well, *Governor*, that would be your decision, would it not?"

Smug satisfaction raised Brude's spirits. He quickly forgot the insults and the condescension of his host. He imagined that he would one day enjoy an amiable camaraderie with Agricola, as well as the social benefits that relationship would bestow upon him.

The following morning, Ailpein's men resumed their surveillance of Brude and his unfortunate companion when they left the Roman fort. Brude schemed on the journey back to camp, formulating his plot to deal with Calach and to achieve the capitulation of the Picts. He would have to maneuver carefully, and wait patiently for the proper opportunities to arise for him to carry out his plan.

The pair made the return journey at a more leisurely pace to accommodate Brude's scheming, and to stage a hunt that would explain Brude's lengthy absence from the Pict camp. Six days after they had left the Roman general, Brude and Bhaltair rode loudly into camp, dragging a bloody stag behind them for all to see.

Ailpein's men returned quietly from the opposite side of the camp, and they rushed to tell Ailpein all that they had seen.

Ailpein's eyes blazed at the news. He had the scouts escort him immediately to Calach's tent.

Before he left the Roman fort, Brude had arranged with Agricola for a detachment of Pretani soldiers to come to the Picts under a flag of truce. They were to request a party of Pict leaders, especially to include Calach, to accompany them to a conference with Agricola. Brude would join the Pictish contingent, and by the end of the meeting, either Brude would have delivered Calach's agreement to the Picts' capitulation, or Calach would be dead.

Within a week, the Pretani detachment arrived as planned. Twenty barbarians dressed as Romans arrived at the Pict camp, under a truce flag and a drenching rain. They were immediately surrounded and pressed close by the razor-sharp tips of Pictish spears. The Pretani captain asked that they be taken to the camp commanders. They were ushered into Calach's command tent.

Calach called for each tribe's chief to join them to receive whatever message the Pretani had brought. While they waited, the captain, called Baelagh, silently assessed Calach. Baelagh nodded silently to each chief as he entered the tent, but he kept his focus tightly on Calach.

While apparently oblivious to Baelagh's attention, Calach noted it well. He knew that he was the main purpose of their visit, and he rightly suspected the connection to Brude's visit with Agricola.

Calach noted with veiled contempt the careful pride with which these warriors wore and maintained their Roman uniforms. Their buckles and buttons gleamed, and their weapons glinted free of the tarnish that was stubbornly abundant in this damp land. Aside from their swarthy Pretanic complexion and longish hair, these men were perfect Roman soldiers.

The sight of them soured Calach's stomach. Island natives clothed as Roman soldiers symbolized for him the betrayal of ancient culture and hard-won independence, in return for the illusion of Roman protection and the fist of Roman rule. Baelagh detected nothing of these thoughts as he searched Calach's expressionless face.

When all the chiefs had arrived, Ailpein called the room to order, and he turned to demand of Baelagh his objective. Calach had resolved not to speak, but rather to let Ailpein act in his stead.

"My general, Agricola, has requested a communion with the leaders of your army," Baelagh said. "He has specifically directed me to stress his desire for a peaceful discussion among honorable men. I am to ask you to accompany me as soon as it is possible for you to do so. He thanks you in advance for honoring him with your presence."

Baelagh met Calach's steady gaze. Ailpein moved to block his line of sight, standing directly in front of Baelagh.

"What motive have we to meet with your Agricola?" Ailpein asked.

Baelagh looked up into Ailpein's serious eyes.

"Peace," he said simply.

"Agricola wants peace?" Ailpein asked.

"He does."

Ailpein laughed.

"On what terms? At what cost to us?"

Baelagh explained that he was not authorized to discuss Agricola's intentions, his motives, or his plans, but only to invite the group to a meeting.

Domhnall grunted and laughed, and moved to stand beside Ailpein. He asked Baelagh about the Romans' troop strength and the positions of their armies. Another clan leader inquired about the strength of Roman reserves to the south in Britannia. Like a beehive disturbed, the room surged into a flurry of intimidating questions.

Baelagh looked frantically toward the door. His heart pounded when he realized that it was heavily guarded, and that the tent was

surrounded by hundreds of painted men, fully armed. He finally
looked to Brude, who sat frozen on his seat in the shadows, away from
Calach.

At long last, Baelagh could take no more. He stood suddenly and
spoke loudly, directly to Calach.

"I am sent to bring you to Agricola. That is all. Agricola wishes to
speak with you." He pointed weakly toward Calach, and the room fell
silent. Calach rose slowly and moved toward Baelagh. Brude tensed.

"Me," Calach said softly. "What business could Agricola possibly
have with me?" Calach shot a glance toward Brude, and then he bore
into Baelagh, who shrugged with a bewildered look.

"I have my orders," Baelagh said. "They're all I know."

"Have the Romans taught the Pretani to lie so well?" Calach
taunted. "To lie, to deceive, and to betray? Is that what they gave you in
return for your heritage?"

"I don't know anything. I swear it," Baelagh protested.

"You swear it? Then you have betrayed your honor as well." Calach
towered directly over Baelagh now. "Do not take me for a fool. We
know of Brude's visit to your general."

Calach's gaze shifted to Brude again, and held there for a moment.

"We know of a plan," Calach continued. "We just don't know what
that plan is. You will tell us now. Do not tell me that you have heard no
rumors, that there has been no talk. Have the Pretani lost their gift for
gossip as well? Tell me what you know."

Baelagh finally relented under Calach's pressure, and in the
presence of so many hostile, threatening faces. He told Calach all he
had heard about Brude's promise to deliver the capitulation of the
Picts, and that Calach would either welcome Roman rule or die
resisting it. Baelagh expressed the Roman belief that only Calach's rage
prevented the Picts from welcoming an alliance with Rome.

When Baelagh finished his declaration, silence reigned once again.
All eyes rested upon Brude, who remained frozen in his seat.

Calach nodded solemnly. He paced slowly, thoughtfully, considering everything that Baelagh had said. His pacing brought him to Brude's side, and he placed a gentle hand upon Brude's flinching, stiffened shoulder.

"Is that so?" Calach finally said. "Is that truly so? We are to agree to capitulation to the Romans?" Calach looked deeply into the eyes of each tribal chief, which were without exception wide with wondrous surprise.

"We shall see," Calach continued. "I shall be going for a while. This room will remain filled only with the will of the Pictish nation, and its twenty Roman visitors. No one will leave this room without the unanimous agreement of the chiefs gathered here. Ailpein speaks for the Caledonii. Domhnall will come with me. When the Pictish nation has agreed together on its position regarding Brude's plan, then Baelagh will come alone to seek me, and bid me return here to hear the decision."

Calach turned to leave.

"I give my word," he added, "that I will honor the will of leaders of the Picts."

Calach and Domhnall left the tent. Calach stared stolidly ahead as they walked through the camp toward Calach's quarters. A soft grunt drew Calach's attention to Domhnall, who wore a wry grin as he slowly shook his head. Calach stared at him, waiting.

"Foolishness," Domhnall spat. Calach said nothing. "For either you or Brude to have the slightest doubt about the will of the Picts is foolishness. I mean no offense to you, my brother, but you know well what the chiefs are about to decide."

"I know, brother. I well know."

Calach and Domhnall had barely reached Calach's tent when Baelagh caught up with them, animated and out of breath.

"They call for you," he gasped. "They bid you return at once. There was hardly a moment's discussion."

Calach turned and motioned Baelagh to lead on. Baelagh noted Calach's utter lack of surprise.

When the trio returned to the tent, the other nineteen Pretani stood huddled under guard. Brude had not moved from his seat, and Bhaltair stood quivering behind him, under guard.

Every tribal chief stood waiting to receive Calach. Each threw his arms around Calach and swore his tribe's undying loyalty, and then everyone returned to their seats. Ailpein remained standing. He turned to face Calach.

"The chiefs wish to speak directly, each and every one, on their position regarding Brude's plan. Each chief speaks for his tribe, and in unison they speak for the Pictish people. We will now hear the will of the Picts." Ailpein took his seat by Calach.

Each chief stood and spoke in turn. Each regarded Brude with contempt as they reiterated their resolve, and the determination of each member of their tribe, to defend their freedom from the Romans at all costs. Each made it clear that they would choose death over life under Roman rule. Each made it clear that their warriors followed Calach willingly, because he epitomized the strength, the honor, and the courage that the Picts had cherished through time. Each chief declared Brude's actions treason, and each was resolute in calling for Brude's death.

Ailpein was the last to speak, and he echoed with eloquence and passion the sentiments of the assembled chiefs. He emphasized the necessity of Brude's execution, as it would clarify for everyone the resolve with which the Picts would defy Roman aggression.

At long last, Calach spoke. He turned in his chair toward Brude, who glared sullenly back at him, and Bhaltair, who stood trembling uncontrollably.

"Treason," Calach said. "This is not my judgment, but that of the chiefs of the nation of the Picts. I agree with it." Calach paused to let the words hang in the air.

"Death," he continued. "This is not my penalty, but that of the rule of our land. You have brought it upon yourselves.

"You, Brude, are the worst of our kind. You have placed your selfish desire for personal gain above the welfare of the tribe that gave you life." Brude tried to speak, but Calach silenced him with a look.

"You, Bhaltair, are the weakest of our kind. In your weakness you have been misled into thinking that you could gain from the betrayal of your clan, your tribe, your blood. You are not worthy of your blood. A man not worthy of his blood does not deserve to live."

Brude shifted in his chair. He began to shake his head vigorously, and his eyes flitted wildly about the room as the reality of his situation set in.

"I went to seek peace," Brude protested, "and to bring prosperity to our people. I went to save lives, and to gain for ourselves the strength and the…the security of the Roman Empire. I went for the good of our people."

His wild eyes seemed on the verge of insanity, and they were focused intensely upon Calach. Two guards moved to restrain him, and they tied his arms securely around the back of the chair. When Brude was secured, Calach replied.

"You went to seek prosperity and power for yourself, and false stature for your own name. You went to sell what you do not own, in return for something you do not deserve. You offered the priceless freedom of your people in exchange for your personal gain. You sought illegitimate authority over them, to be granted to you by a foreign invader. You did so because you failed…repeatedly…to earn such an honor in the Pictish way. Now you will pay for your dishonor in the Pictish way."

"You can't do this," wailed Brude. "You have no right! I was trying to save our people from your blundering!"

Calach waved Brude's protest away and shook his head.

"I will not be the one to execute you. This is not between you and me. Your transgression was against all Picts, and your dishonor against all men. It matters not at all who is to be your executioner. He shall be chosen from among the chiefs. To me, you are already dead."

Calach turned away from Brude and said no more. Brude's bellow of rage was heard throughout the camp, cut short by the blow of a guard's fist against the side of his head.

Despite the flag of truce under which the Pretani had entered the Pict camp, the chiefs considered that they should die for their part in Brude's deception. Calach felt that they should honor the truce flag, but he agreed to leave the Pretani soldiers' fate in the hands of the chiefs. The Pretani were detained while the chiefs debated their fate.

Near noon the following day, the chiefs broke from their debate long enough to carry out Brude's execution. Ailpein was chosen, and he seemed to welcome the honor. The manner in which he chose to carry it out was ceremoniously symbolic, and to most observers, appropriately dreadful.

Brude was bound to the trunk of a sturdy tree, and denied the blindfold for which he plaintively begged. Ailpein stood in front of him, preparing to fulfill his task. Calach approached, touching Ailpein's shoulder. Calach motioned Ailpein to step aside for a moment, and Ailpein dutifully complied.

Calach took his place in front of Brude. He stared hard into Brude's eyes for a long moment before he spoke, quietly, almost mournfully.

"I have long known of the contempt you hold for me. You have always wished me ill. I know that if you had your way, I would now be dead, and you would command this army. And now perhaps you finally understand that that could have never been so."

Brude glared back defiantly.

"I chose you to be my second in command for a reason. I respected and trusted your skills in war, but I never trusted your loyalty to me for a moment. You have spoken more often than you should have, and to too many that you should not have.

"My alliance with you strengthened the unity of our army. That unity alone would allow us the strength to drive these Romans from our land. Your betrayal by its very nature threatened that unity. And now, because of your betrayal, only your death will preserve the unity of this army."

"Your misjudgments will destroy your precious army," Brude growled. "Your foolishness will be the end of you."

"I have been staggered by my personal loss," Calach conceded after a moment, "and shaken by my error in tactical judgment. But I am neither broken nor defeated. You have miscalculated the affliction of my grief, and you have brought this fate upon yourself."

Calach turned and walked a short distance away, from where he would watch in silence, his face filled with darkness, as Ailpein carried out Brude's sentence.

Ailpein resumed his position in front of Brude. He drew his dagger and pronounced Brude's treason against each of the Pictish tribes, and indeed, against each Pict.

Ailpein began to shout the names of each of the twenty tribes, pausing after each to draw his dagger's razor edge across a different place on Brude's stiffening body. Each cut was deep enough to cause anguish, but not collapse.

"Smertae," Ailpein announced, starting with the tribe of Brude's birth. He cut deeply across Brude's belly, below the navel. Brude cried out as blood streamed down his trembling thighs.

"Novantii," Ailpein said, and he slashed Brude's right forearm.

"Venicones," Ailpein shouted, while he cut deeply into Brude's left shoulder.

After nineteen tribes had been named, and nineteen non-fatal but excruciating wounds inflicted, Brude's head rolled from side to side as he moaned in agony. His life was draining slowly from his tattered body.

Ailpein finally grasped the hair on the top of Brude's head and pulled his face close to his own. Ailpein held the tip of his dagger to the hollow of Brude's throat, just above where the clavicles met the sternum. Ailpein took a deep breath and roared a final name.

"*Caledonii!*" he cried. Ailpein pushed the dagger slowly, until its hilt rested firmly against the slippery skin of Brude's gushing throat. Blood foamed from the wound as Brude struggled in vain to cry out. His body sagged as what remained of his life ebbed away.

Brude's lifeless body was cut down from the tree, beheaded, and then torn to pieces, one for each of the tribes he had attempted to betray. The pieces of his body were strewn across a nearby bog, thrown far and wide.

Bhaltair was simply beheaded and dumped into the bog, his headless body weighted by stones, to rest among what remained of the traitor he had chosen to follow.

"A fate befitting a lowly weakling pig," Ailpein had said as Bhaltair's body sank into the bog.

Calach turned to walk quickly away, but he was intercepted by one of the guards who were assigned to the Pretani. They spoke for a moment and then turned and walked toward the place where the captives were held.

The Pretani were crowded into a cage made of birch logs, lashed close and sturdy to prevent escape. The cage was surrounded by painted, spear-bearing guards. Calach and his escort approached the cage, and Baelagh motioned to them.

"What do you want?" Calach asked.

"I understand that you will probably kill us," Baelagh said.

"That has not been decided," Calach answered.

"Nevertheless, I couldn't blame you."

"What do you want?"

"To join you. Most of us, anyway. If your chiefs were to decide to allow us to return home, we would prefer to stay here, and to fight for you."

"Of course. What else would you say, in your current position?"

"Yes, that is true, of course," Baelagh conceded. "But we have seen in you and your people something that has long been lost in ours. You have inspired us with your strength and your ideals. If your decision is to kill us, we will take our own lives willingly, with honor. I ask you now to let that be so, should it come to that."

Calach nodded thoughtfully.

"But if the chiefs decide to set us free under our flag of truce, I request that you allow those of us who would do so to stay with you here. And I will ask only one other thing."

"Yes?"

"Speak nothing of my request to anyone until after the decision has been made. Do not bring it to the chiefs. Until our fate is rightfully decided, I ask you to keep my request between us."

"Then why ask it of me now?" Calach asked.

"So that either way you would know what you have done for me. I remember now what it meant to be Pretani, and proud. I remember now that both of those words meant the same thing. I want to regain what we have lost, what you carry in your heart, what makes you the warrior you are, and what prevents you from becoming a lesser thing. That's what you've given me, and I wanted you to know that, come what may."

Calach looked into Baelagh's eyes appreciatively. He suddenly pitied his plight, and the condition into which his people had fallen. Calach tried to grasp the feeling of such a loss, but could not. He nodded slightly and held out his hand. Baelagh grasped it.

"You have my word," Calach said.

"And you have mine," Baelagh answered.

Later that afternoon, Lachann, chief of the Novantii, approached Calach with news from the chiefs. The chiefs had finally decided that Calach was right, and that they should honor the Pretani's flag of truce, even though it had been flown in deception. They agreed that the true deception was perpetrated by Brude, who had paid its price, and not by the pawns in his ruse. Lachann noted that Calach's sense of honor continued to inspire his brethren chiefs, and he expressed their regard for his wisdom in the matter.

Calach nodded, and he then revealed to Lachann Baelagh's private request, as further evidence of the wisdom of their decision. Calach marveled aloud at the Pretani detachment's willingness to take their own lives in honor of the Picts' ruling.

Calach asked Lachann to meet again with the chiefs to approve an invitation, to be formally presented by Ailpein, for those Pretani who wished it to join the Caledonii tribe.

In the evening, a feast was prepared. The Picts would celebrate their victory over Brude's attempt to betray them. They would loudly proclaim their continued resolve to resist the Roman invasion, and they would more loudly reaffirm their loyalty to their chosen leader. Afterward, the Pretani would hear of the decision on their fate.

Ailpein called for silence among the camp. He motioned for the Pretani to be brought forth, and for Calach to declare their destiny. Baelagh and his men stood silently in formation before the gathering of chiefs, who betrayed no hint of their verdict. Calach stood and quietly faced the Pretani.

"You came here to deceive us. You came on the orders of your superiors, but you came here just the same. You came as enemies of our people, to draw our people into the slavery into which you yourselves have descended. You came to assist in our destruction, and some have argued fairly and justly for your death."

Some of the Pretani nodded in solemn acknowledgement.

"Others have argued that just men should honor a truce flag, even if it was carried in fraud and duplicity.

"But for one compelling thing, I would look coldly upon your execution, had my chiefs called for it, for I hold their word to be just.

"However, the chiefs of our tribes have chosen to spare your lives, and to honor your flag of truce."

Most of the Pretani heaved heavy sighs of relief, and all looked with wonder at the gathered chiefs. Baelagh, the captain of the Pretani, held his head high and beamed heartfelt admiration for the man to whom he had just now sworn his life.

"You are free to go," Calach announced.

"However," he continued, "there is the matter of that one compelling thing. One of you, a man of honor and courage, came to me earlier in confidence and gave me a secret vow. I know that he spoke for many of you when he did, and in doing so he earned my respect.

"Your captain has rediscovered that which was taken from you long ago, something for which he is once again willing to die. He has discovered anew that which drives us to conquer those who presume to enslave us. He has remembered the pride of the free, and he has reclaimed it for himself. He, and each of you who choose it now, shall have it from this day forward."

Calach motioned to Ailpein, who rose as Calach resumed his seat.

"You are all free to go," Ailpein declared. "You may leave as soon as you choose. You are also free to stay, on the condition that you swear your loyalty, upon your life.

"For those who choose to stay, I have the honor of accepting you into the Caledonii tribe. You will live and serve as Caledonii, free men in all respects but one – your loyalty is unconditional, and the failure of it will be your death. This you are not free to choose."

Many of the Pretani nodded among themselves, considering the gesture generous.

"Those who wish, come forward now, and swear the oath of a Caledone," Ailpein commanded.

Thirteen of the twenty came forward. They prepared to receive their first Caledonii mark, the inverted crescent tattoo, with the representation of female fertility at its center, and a broken arrow in the form of a "V" superimposed, its ends extending up and to either side of the inverted crescent.

The marking was ancient and meaningful: it represented the peace their ancestors had made with the Scoti and with their forbidding new home, and the importance of the miracle of feminine fertility to the perpetuation of their people.

Seven of the Pretani chose to return to the south, some apologetically explaining their obligation to family they had left behind. Two appeared to harbor contempt for the Picts, and for the Pretani who chose to stay. These, Ailpein chose for a special mission. He pulled them aside and into a nearby tent.

Once inside, Ailpein presented the two with a package, and a letter from Baelagh, to carry back with them to the Roman fort. The package was wrapped thickly and securely in deerskin, and it was sealed and marked to be opened only in the presence of Agricola.

The seven Pretani departed early the following day.

When the seven Pretani arrived at the Roman fort, they were taken immediately to report to Agricola. They presented the package and the letter, and stood silently awaiting Agricola's command. Agricola opened the letter with a bewildered look.

As he read Baelagh's letter, Agricola's eyes grew wide, and his mouth hung slack. Baelagh had requested that Agricola accept his decision to remain among the Picts, and he had begged Agricola not to hold the seven accountable for the failure of their mission. Baelagh assured Agricola that each of the seven had sworn their allegiance to Rome as they had left the camp.

Agricola stared blankly at the letter for a moment. Finally, he looked sternly at the returned Pretani and demanded an explanation of what had transpired at the Pict camp.

"Of course, sir," one ventured. "I might suggest, however, that you open the package first." He said this with a hint of trepidation; the group had correctly guessed the contents of Ailpein's package.

Agricola motioned to an aide to open the package.

The aide unwrapped the layers of skin. The inner layer was caked with congealed blood, and the aide looked to Agricola with growing concern. He finally pulled the last layer of skins away from a clump of bloody, matted hair, and Brude's head came loose and landed with a thump on Agricola's precious oak table. Its glazed eyes stared at Agricola in astonishment.

"They knew," the Pretani said. "We never had a chance. There was not the slightest chance that the Picts would come in. They will never come in."

In spite of Baelagh's request, Agricola had the seven confined for the failure of their mission. He thought that he had detected in the Pretani's voice the faintest hint of admiration for the Picts, and he would not permit such sentiment the slightest chance of spreading through his camp. Agricola quietly ordered a captain to carry out the immediate and secret execution of the returned Pretani, and to spread word throughout the camp of the ambush and slaughter of his delegation by the intractable Picts.

Agricola knew that there was no hope of peaceful capitulation or assimilation of the Picts. He knew that this battle would rage until one side or the other was overcome. He cursed softly to himself, knowing that the odds leaned considerably against his success.

19

Hunting the Twentieth

OVER THE FOLLOWING WEEKS, random Roman scouting parties were ambushed and destroyed with impunity. Others were allowed to roam freely, returning to camp with nothing to report, with a few exceptions of sightings of painted warriors watching them from the hills.

The observers seemed to vanish as soon as they were seen, without a skirmish. The effect was as intended: the Romans never knew if they were to be attacked or allowed to pass unchallenged. Confusion and the disconcerting fear of unpredictability increased among the Roman ranks.

Finally, on a crisp, clear morning, a Roman scout party came upon a glen surrounded by open, rolling hills. The hills were ringed by a thick wall of tall, ancient trees. A sight ahead of them stopped them in their tracks as they entered the glen.

Up ahead, in the middle of the glen, stood a dozen unarmed Picts. They stood fast, in stolid defiance. After momentary hesitation, the Romans began to advance. They intended to slaughter the Picts.

Ailpein stepped forward and raised his hand, signaling the Romans to stop. They slowed, but continued forward, menacing. Ailpein stretched both hands to the sky and began to turn in circles, indicating the hills surrounding the glen.

Looking up, the scouts were stunned by the sight of thousands of Picts in a ring about the glen, just outside the tree line, with weapons raised. They were men with spears and women archers, half-naked and painted in the Pictish tradition. There were thousands of archers, their bows drawn and focused on the scouts. The sunlight glinted off of a sea of axes, swords, and spears. The Romans knew that they were doomed.

Ailpein lowered his arms and crossed them on his chest. He glared at the Romans in defiance. The scouts began to retreat in the direction from which they had come. The Picts remained motionless, allowing them to retreat. The centurion in command gave the order, and the scouts turned full about and fled, expecting the sea of Picts to fall upon them at any moment. But as the centurion took one last look behind him, he saw that the Picts had vanished into the trees. The glen was abandoned.

As the scouts made their way back to the fort, the centurion began to wonder if he had imagined the entire incident.

When the scouts reported to Agricola, the general smiled with grim satisfaction. At last, he knew where to find the Picts. He knew where the battle would occur.

He would attack at dawn, with all of his available might. The thought never occurred to him that Calach had carefully chosen the time and the place for his next battle.

The Romans arrived in full force before dawn at the deserted glen. Agricola sent scouts across the empty fields for signs of the enemy presence. They found none.

As the sun rose on the silence, Agricola swore beneath his breath. He was losing his patience with these damnable barbarians. The legion stood over twelve thousand strong, growing irritable and restless under the glare of the strengthening sun.

Agricola sent reluctant scouts up the hills and into the trees, half-expecting to hear their screams when they encountered the hidden Picts. The scouts soon returned, unharmed and visibly relieved.

Agricola decided to push on. The legion advanced through the glen, and followed the road as it rose into the hills ahead. They marched for an hour, expecting to come upon their quarry at every turn.

Another hour passed, and the exasperated legion found itself in the middle of another glen. This was a deeper valley, surrounded by steeply rising hills, which were also ringed by a thick wall of trees. The scouts repeated their search, hunting fruitlessly among the trees for signs of Picts.

Sensing another episode of barbarian trickery, Agricola decided with great annoyance to turn back.

The legion soon passed back through the first glen, and continued toward the fort. To a man, the Romans were frustrated by their failure to engage the Picts. They marched on swearing and shaking their heads.

Upon their return to the fort, the advance scouts called to the sentries to open the gates for the returning legion. As the gates opened, the scouts were astonished by an outlandish scene. The fort was littered with the bodies of all who had remained behind. In a moment, Agricola arrived and flew into a violent but impotent rage.

"These damned barbarians!" Agricola bellowed. He flew off his horse and stormed into the fort. "Bastards!" he screamed. He turned and walked furiously outside the fort and shook his fist at the trees. "Come and fight us like men, you bastards!"

Agricola realized that he was losing his composure, and he caught himself, feeling foolish. He walked back into the fort to face yet another, more incredible shock.

The fort was suddenly filled with leering Picts, who seemed to have materialized from nowhere. Thousands had emerged from tents throughout the fort, and now they stood massed against the Romans at the gates. Most of the legion had remained outside, waiting to enter.

The Picts did not hesitate. They fell upon those that had entered the fort, screaming their terrible war cries. Pipes wailed and drums pounded and the bulk of the Roman legion pressed into the gates and piled upon itself, trying to get inside and to the battle.

Those that succeeded were quickly killed. The gates were soon blocked by a mountain of bodies, making it increasingly difficult for those outside to enter the fort.

The soldiers outside the fort heard a loud and victorious cry from within. Several dozen soldiers scaled the wall in time to see the horde of Picts disappearing into the back of the fort. They pursued them, and watched in dismay as they disappeared through an enormous breach in the back wall of the fort.

The Picts had demonstrated once again their cunning, their remarkable mobility, and their ability to melt away from the Romans' sight. When he finally made his way inside the fort, Agricola stood fuming, angrily massaging his temples with the fingers of his left hand. He knew he had to engage these barbarians in open battle, immediately.

Toward evening, Agricola met with his command. In the morning they would break camp, and march north once again. They would march until the met resistance, or until night fell. They would search until they found and destroyed their elusive enemy.

The next morning the Twentieth Legion arrived once again at the glen. They halted and sent scouts to the edges of the trees, again to search for signs of the Picts. They returned after a quarter of an hour with nothing to report. As they prepared to march on, Agricola caught sight of movement up ahead. The forward scouts shouted as they too saw the band of Picts disappearing into the distance ahead.

The Twentieth Legion mobilized in hot pursuit.

20

Battle in the Glen

THE TWENTIETH LEGION marched for several miles until they came once again to the mouth of the deep valley where Agricola had sensed ambush the day before. The Picts had maintained their distance ahead of the Romans, moving just slowly enough to remain within their sight. Agricola was well aware that their speed was intentional. While he was curious about their motives, he was more intent on the battle that lay ahead.

When the legion entered the valley, they once again found it empty. Agricola signaled the legion to halt. He sat upon his steed searching the hills, and the scouts fanned out to investigate them.

Just then, a band of several hundred Picts approached on horseback from the far side of the valley. They moved slowly and steadily toward the Romans, without a hint of concern. The Romans came to attention at the sight. Agricola signaled with a raised fist – the signal to hold position.

Agricola then saw Picts emerging from the surrounding trees above and all around them, in the same manner as they had two days earlier, sending the scout detachment scurrying back to the fort in alarm.

The Picts on the road continued their advance.

Agricola observed the leader at the head of the approaching Picts. His reddish-brown hair was matted and wild, and it framed a chiseled, painted, and tensely glowering face. With his head tilted slightly forward, Calach glared at Agricola through steely eyes.

Calach and his companions stopped thirty yards from the Romans, and sat quietly, as if assessing them.

Finally, Calach spurred his horse into a leisurely walk toward Agricola. A Novantii tribesman accompanied him to translate. The Novantii warrior had spent several years as a prisoner of the Romans, and he had a working grasp of their language.

Calach drew close to Agricola. He regarded him intently, staring into his eyes. The effect on Agricola was unsettling. Agricola sensed an innate power in the man, and an inexorable sureness in his manner.

When Calach finally spoke, Agricola noted odd warmth that seemed inherent in his voice, which was incongruous with the angry harshness of his words.

"You have made a grave mistake," Calach hissed. The Novantii translated.

Agricola said nothing. He waited for Calach to continue.

"You will die here today." With that, Calach wheeled his horse to return to his men.

"Wait!" Agricola shouted. Calach stopped, turning back to face him. "I will discuss terms."

The Novantii snickered as he translated Agricola's words for Calach. Calach peered intently into Agricola's eyes, bemused.

"*Condicionem?*" Calach spat the Latin word, as though it were dirt in his mouth. "I did not come here to discuss terms. I came here to look into your eyes, and to tell you that you will die here today. There are no terms, except that you will leave or die." The Novantii translated those words with great pride.

Agricola paled slightly, and sat staring.

"Prepare to die," Calach said as he spun his horse around again and rode off. The Novantii laughed softly and snarled at the Roman before he turned to follow Calach.

For over an hour the Romans stood ready in the sun as it climbed higher over the valley. The Picts stood silent, unmoving, on the ridge surrounding the Romans. Just as Agricola began to wonder why they didn't attack, he understood.

They did not want to meet him on the field. They were waiting for him to attack, uphill against their superior position, and in the meantime they were allowing the Romans to bake in the sweltering sun.

Agricola resolved to wait them out and force them to come to him.

As if they were reading Agricola's mind, the Pictish archers suddenly came to the fore. Of almost eight thousand warriors, Agricola estimated fully a quarter stood ready to loose their darts. Agricola shouted the order to cover against the arrows.

A moment later, the sky seemed to cloud over as thousands of Pictish arrows left their bows. They sailed high and arced swiftly into the legion's midst. The drumbeat of arrows thudding into upraised shields filled the valley, providing a prelude to the pipes that began a low drone through the hills. Pictish drums joined the tune as the archers prepared another volley.

Agricola knew that they couldn't simply stand there in an endless shower of screaming darts. He would be forced into action, just as the Picts had planned. After two more volleys he ordered the charge up the hill.

The Picts held the strength of position, and they used it well to repel the first attack. In the meantime, a division of Pictish chariots moved into position behind the Romans, cutting them off from retreat. Calach was pleased to see that his strategy had worked. The Romans were trapped on an uphill field.

The chariots closed in on the Romans, and the warriors on the ridge began to push downward, closing the legion within a tightening noose. The Romans fought unabated to drive the Picts back.

Suddenly, Calach noted that the chariots seemed to stall, and those at the rear appeared to be turning around. He was surprised to realize that they were under attack from behind.

Eight thousand more Romans had arrived from the south; Agricola had sent to lower Britannia for reinforcements when he realized that the Ninth Legion had been vanquished. There were now close to twenty thousand Romans. The Picts were outnumbered by nearly two to one.

Calach quickly signaled retreat, and the Picts moved to salvage the chariot forces in the process. The chariots were caught between the rescued Twentieth and the arriving reserves, and they were taking significant losses. Calach focused the bulk of his army on opening a northern escape route for the chariots.

The Picts took significant, though not crippling losses before their retreat was complete. As before, they melted into the woods, leaving the Romans astonished by the ease and efficiency with which they moved. As quickly as the reinforcements had arrived, the battle was over and the Romans were alone on the field.

Each side had taken heavy losses. The battle had been evenly matched until the Roman auxiliaries arrived. As the dust settled, the legion and the auxiliaries moved into formation for a retreat to the south for the night.

Later that evening, in the solace of his tent, Calach struggled. He struggled as he struggled every night now, to contain and to quell the bitterness and despair that had consumed him since Fiona was snatched from his life. In the darkness of despair, he felt that he was losing sight of his mission. He was giving in to the desire for vicious revenge. He no longer cared that Romans were trampling his sacred ground. He only wanted the taste of their blood as compensation for what he had lost.

These things contradicted everything Calach had ever held in his heart. Alone in his tent, his father's words and Girom's face haunted him, taunting him, and begging him to heed them once again. Calach struggled to let go of the fury that had captured and now threatened to imprison his spirit. But the fury was driving him now, and in that he recognized the death of yet one more thing that he had long cherished.

Calach resolved that he would find victory over his terrible affliction.

21

'Mons Graupius'

AS MORNING BROKE over the eastern hills, Calach stood gazing out over the land, admiring the beauty of the cobalt blue of the western mountains. He imagined standing there with Fiona; it occurred to him that she may have loved this land even more than he did.

She had completed his world, and he thought that paradise could not have been much better than this land with Fiona in it. Calach spent each morning in this manner, trying in vain to recapture a sliver of the joy with which she had infused his life.

Through the mist of his reverie, Calach heard a commotion at the edge of the camp. He turned to see a crowd of his men escorting a group of Pretani auxiliaries toward the command tent. Calach moved to join them at the tent. He called for Ailpein and Domhnall to join him.

Ailpein, Domhnall, and Calach entered the tent to question the messengers from the Twentieth Legion. They came under another flag of truce. They could have faced interrogation and summary death, since the last truce flag had been nothing more than a devious ruse, but these Pretani came with a personal message for Calach, from Agricola.

The Roman governor had requested a meeting with Calach, not to discuss terms for battle or capitulation, but just to talk – a conversation between two men. The Pretani seemed to think that Calach had made quite an impression on Agricola, who was exceedingly curious about him.

Calach stormed out of his chair in contempt.

"I am not a curiosity for him to inspect," Calach growled. "Who does this pig think he is, summoning me to his feet?" He threw a leather helmet across the tent, startling the Pretani messengers. "And you," he said to the Pretani, wheeling toward them, "you continue to fight for them! What has become of your honor? Have you no dignity at all?"

The Pretani looked at the ground in abject shame. Calach shook his head in disgust. Everyone watched in silence as Calach paced.

"Tell him to come to me!" Calach finally shouted. The other Picts looked up in surprise. "Tell him that if he doesn't come to me, then I will certainly come to him, and he will surely die. He has two days. Then it's done."

Calach dismissed the Pretani with his message for the Roman.

Calach spent the rest of the day and all of that evening circulating throughout the camp, speaking to groups of warriors in the manner to which they had grown accustomed.

Several days later, Calach again spent the sunrise with his thoughts of his wife, looking for her in the mists that had settled into the valley in the night. He spoke to her in silent words that soothed his mind and calmed his soul. He longed for her tender touch, and he wondered if even she could ease this enormous splinter of hatred from his heart.

Once again, his reverie was broken by the sound of commotion in the wakening camp. Today's arrivals were Roman, and not Pretani. Calach turned to watch the approach of the Governor of Britannia. He motioned to the intercepting guards to bring Agricola into the command tent, and then he paused for one more moment with Fiona before he joined them.

When Calach entered his command tent, Agricola was standing in the center of the room with four of his centurions and an aide by his side. The centurions looked arrogant and stiff, and the aide seemed nervous and shy. Calach noted the polish of the Romans' attire, and the pride with which they wore their shining insignia. He took a long moment to observe Agricola, estimating his stature and depth.

In Agricola, he saw a thoughtful man. He did not appear to be ill tempered or crass, but rather practical, logical, and disciplined. Calach sat, and he motioned for Agricola to do the same.

As Agricola sat, the nervous aide began to unpack a leather satchel, removing a roll of papyrus and an ornate quill pen. Calach watched him carefully, and then he looked questioningly at Agricola.

"What is he doing?" Calach asked. Sioltach the Pretani Selgovae translated, repeating the question in Latin for Agricola.

"He will record what happens here today," Agricola explained.

Sioltach explained to Calach with great mirth how Romans liked to record everything they said, and did, and thought, so that their greatness would be remembered for all time.

Sioltach could not stifle a laugh at Calach's bewildered reaction. This was something no Pict would ever think to do; actions or words worth remembering were never forgotten, while everything else was left in the past where it belonged. Sioltach was deeply amused by the stark contrast between the two men. Calach stared at Agricola and his scribe, mystified.

"You do not summon me," Calach stated. His anger was evident through the evenness of his voice. Agricola said nothing. "You have invaded my land, and you presume to summon me to your feet. Who do you think you are, and what kind of dog do you think me to be?"

"I did not think you would allow me to depart your tent with my life," Agricola said.

"You thought rightly," Calach replied. "So, why are you here now?"

"I want a peaceful solution."

"A peaceful solution to what?" Calach asked. "To the rape and plunder you have brought here to my land? The solution is simple and clear, and there is nothing more to discuss. Leave, or you will all die. That is all."

"Perhaps we can make peace," Agricola offered. "We have made peace with the Pretani." He looked up at Sioltach as he said that. Sioltach answered first, before translating for Calach.

"You have made slaves of the Pretani," he hissed. Calach let Sioltach's response stand.

"Most of the Pretani enjoy the comforts of Roman citizenship, and they live in peace," Agricola countered.

"Peace and comfort," Calach repeated. "We have lived here in peace and comfort for thousands of years. You offer us nothing we did not already have in abundance long before your Romulus murdered his brother."

Agricola raised his eyebrows. "You know of Romulus, then?"

"You think me a stupid animal," Calach said in contempt. "Your Roman arrogance renders you foolish. Is it so hard for you to believe that there are men of wit outside your so-called empire?" Agricola was silent. "Why are you here, Roman? To spread your arrogance and foolishness over my land, too?"

Agricola was struggling to read this man, to find a chink in his armor that would enable him to get through, and to get what he wanted. What he wanted was simple enough: to finish the task of bringing the whole of the Britannic Island under Roman rule, as peaceably and with as few casualties as possible. He was realizing that it would probably not happen peaceably here.

"I have come to accomplish the inevitable," Agricola said. "The empire that I am helping to build will one day stretch to the farthest ends of the earth. I had hoped to do my part to make that happen peaceably, sparing those we hope will join us in civilizing the world."

Calach said nothing, but sat quietly, staring into Agricola's eyes. Agricola could see that the Pict's mind was working, that he was considering Agricola's words. Agricola continued.

"My Emperor has sent me here to bring the whole of the Britannic Island into the realm of his Empire. I will not disappoint him. You will one day find that it is a good thing to be part of the Roman Empire. There are many advantages to being a part of the greatest power on earth."

"There are many advantages to being free," Calach said.

"As a Roman you would be free," Agricola insisted.

Calach looked at Agricola with disdain. He curbed his desire to kill the man, knowing the value of hearing him out. Calach understood well that the more men spoke, the more they gave away, and the more they listened, the more they gained.

"Perhaps you should know the possibilities," Agricola continued. "If you continue to resist, many more of you will die. If you defeat my army today, twice as many will replace it tomorrow. The day will finally come when your people will submit to Rome. The only question is how many will be left to submit. Those that do will have lost much, and they will curse your name for all time."

Calach listened.

"On the other hand, you could consider this. If we agree to peace, Rome will treat your people well. They will be welcomed into our arms. They will call themselves Romans and go freely wherever they choose. This land would become known as the Britannic Province of Rome, and you could be known as its king."

"King," Calach repeated. The word was bitter in his mouth. His eyes narrowed.

"I have the authority to crown you king of the Britannic Island," Agricola said. "You would rule this land, reporting only to me. This is the best you can do for your people, and they would praise your name for all time."

Agricola sat quietly then, to let Calach consider his words. He imagined that he had just offered this barbarian more than he had ever desired. He could not have been more wrong.

"So you would make me a king," Calach finally said, feigning astonished appreciation. "I would be much indebted to you then, I suppose." Agricola nodded a curt half-acknowledgement. Knowing nothing of the man to whom he spoke, Agricola still thought wrongly that Calach was considering the offer.

"King over what domain?" Calach asked. "Over a nation of people betrayed, robbed of all that they prize, and sold into slavery to mongrels by the very man to whom they entrusted their cause?" Calach stroked his close shaven beard. "How could I refuse that bribe?

"My dear Roman," he continued, "you disappoint me even more than I thought you would." Calach placed a tender hand upon the head of his faithful deer hound, which lay dutifully beside him, looking up at the Roman with sorrowful eyes. "There is more honor in this faithful hound than there is to be found in a thousand men like you."

Calach felt his rage boiling over the dam he was trying desperately to maintain.

"You have violated our peace, unprovoked," he continued. "You have wounded my brother and murdered my wife, so that your emperor might think you worthy. I would have thought you worthy simply because you exist. Why are you thought less by the very man for whom you would steal my life? Do you not think on these things?

"Who do you think you are, coming here, invading my land, raping and killing women and children, and then offering me something that will never be yours to give? What kind of people are you? I would sooner cut my own throat than deliver my people to be your slaves."

"They would not be slaves," Agricola protested. "As Roman citizens, they would be free. All Roman citizens are free."

"No Roman citizen is free. You yourself are not free," Calach snarled.

"I'm not free? I command one tenth of the Roman army. I have more power than do most living men. How can you say that I am not free?"

Calach was taken aback by Agricola's remark on the size of the Roman army. He had been certain that the legions in Britannia were only a small part of it. He began to realize the true extent of the impact he had had on the Romans over the past years, and to understand the real reason Agricola was here in his tent. He was tempted to kill Agricola on the spot and launch an immediate attack upon what was left of the Britannic legions. But he knew that that would only draw more Romans to his land.

"You are free?" asked Calach. "You call yourself free? Then you do not know freedom. Tell me this, great Roman: what happens to you when you return home to report that you have failed here?" Agricola winced at the thought.

"Only a slave can enslave; slavery is an abomination to men whose hearts are truly free. Tell me you are not a slave to your ambition, and to your emperor. Tell me that your emperor is not a slave to his own greed. Tell me that your entire civilization is not in bondage to itself, and to its endless lust for power and wealth and blood. Your empire is driven to dash itself against the rocks of endless war, in a vain attempt to satisfy its lust."

Calach stood. His anger was surfacing, and he felt suddenly seized by the demons he had been struggling to contain. Sioltach stared at Calach in admiration as he quickly translated his words.

"Why have you lost one legion, soon to be followed by another? Look, and see! Your soldiers are wide-eyed Roman lads, fighting beside non-Romans who were your enemies longer than they have been your slaves. They are bewildered by a strange and frightening land.

They are bound to you not by loyalty, but by fear, and when their fear ends, only hatred will remain.

"For all of your pomp, you have none of what inspires men to victory. Your soldiers fight for nothing but the glory of an empire that has crushed their own nations and tribes. They have no wives to inspire them, and no parents to mock them should they shrink from battle. They have no country, or if they do it is not Rome, and it is in ruins.

"We fight by choice, to a man. Every man you see here is free: free to go and tend to his home, or to stay here with me, and fight. You see that they choose to fight. They fight because they have never known tyranny such as yours. They have always been free. We are the last free men in a world that Rome has consumed in its greed. You have spread robbery, butchery, and rape over the world, and in your arrogance you call that 'Empire'. You spread desolation wherever you go, and you lie and call it peace."

Agricola paled. He was certain that he would die at the hands of this man whose spirit he could not comprehend. Calach continued, pacing.

"You have conquered nations and made them slaves. And now you intend to conquer us. We have no wealth to offer your empire. We have only our honor and pride, the likes of which you would never abide. To succeed here, you will be compelled to kill us all. If you fail in that, then the might of Rome will be broken, and behind you lay your unprotected villages ruled by gray-haired men. Who will protect them from our revenge when you are gone? Do you think that our vengeance will fade? No, General. You have no choice but to turn and leave. Your empire ends at this border, and this border it will never exceed. You cannot win this war."

"I cannot leave," Agricola said in a slightly weakened voice. "I will not report to my Emperor that I have abandoned my mission for fear of you. I would rather die."

"Then you shall." Calach prepared to dismiss his guest.

"Calach," Ailpein broke in. He leaned close to Calach and whispered to him for a moment. Calach arose and nodded to Agricola.

"Wait here," Calach commanded the general. Calach motioned for Domhnall to join him and Ailpein, and the three men walked out of the tent. Calach's faithful hound remained by Calach's empty chair, staring at Agricola with what the general imagined to be a look of heartfelt pity.

Outside, the three men talked for a long while. Agricola contemplated his predicament, feeling trapped. He did not want to continue a costly campaign that he could most assuredly lose. He also could not simply give in to this man. He searched in vain for options. Finally, the three men returned, and Calach offered him the only viable one.

"You will retreat. Every last Roman will leave our land or die," Calach said firmly, and then he paused as he took his seat. Calach glanced at Agricola's scribe, who was busily taking notes. Nodding in his direction, he continued. "You will record for your posterity the great battle that took place here this day."

Agricola looked at Calach in confusion. He was about to speak when Calach waved him to silence.

"You have come here in great numbers and strength," Calach continued. "You were badly outnumbered, but our courage was no match for your might. We have foolishly challenged the pride of the Roman Empire, and you have taught us the error of our ways. We retreated into the hills, having lost fully a third of our number. You have vanquished us. Our land is yours to roam freely if you wish, but for the moment you do not wish that. You plan to return some day to install a proper Roman government over the land. So will say your report."

As Sioltach translated Calach's words, the scribe looked up in dismay, first to Calach, and then to Agricola, whose mouth hung slack.

Calach smiled grimly and said, "I'll have to kill a number of your men, of course, or you will have no casualties to report." His eyes twinkled at the thought, and he laughed. Agricola swore to himself that he could never understand this strange man. Calach's face turned serious once more.

"Go and tell your emperor that you have won, that this island is his, and that we are no longer a threat. Give him his fantasy, for that is all it shall be. We care not whether the world believes you. We know that it will never be so, and so do you. And you will see that neither you, nor any Roman, will ever return to this land.

"But you will retreat. You will go back the way you came, until you have returned far south of the Tweed. The Pretani have accepted your yoke, so return to them, and come here no more. For you, this land is forever cursed. If a man of you should return, or even venture close, we will kill him without hesitation or mercy. If an army comes near, we will destroy it. If your emperor sends governors to rule us, we will kill them and attack your towns."

Calach pointed at the scribe.

"You see, you are also slaves to your posterity. You are compelled to show your greatness to generations not yet born. Why do you care? We care nothing for what others think of us. We care nothing for what history will say of us. We care only for what the world is, and not for what it appears to be. You are only free when you can walk through your life unfettered by such concerns. And you Romans will never be free."

After lengthy discussion, Calach and Agricola solidified their understanding of Calach's terms, and in the year that followed, Agricola did much to honor the truce. He pulled his army back, and led no more raids into the north. The line that separated the Picts from the Romans and everyone else to its south would remain for all time a border, the crossing of which would ever be regarded as an act of war.

Agricola was soon called back to Rome and given another governorship, only to finally learn well the stark truth of Calach's words. He would be murdered by his emperor out of jealousy over the very victory he had "won" for him. And the Picts remained united as a newly federated nation, unbroken by the Roman mace.

22

Lasting Peace?

OVER THE NEXT THREE decades, the Picts solidified their newfound unity while enjoying relative freedom from Roman expansion. They neither knew nor cared about the events in Rome that had distracted the Romans from their Britannic campaign, but they were certain the reprieve was temporary and that they would face the legions again.

Every now and then, a Roman patrol ventured north and disappeared into the mists of Caledonia. Less frequently, a small invasion force would follow a lost patrol, also to disappear. Such incursions were always followed by punishing raids by the Picts, often as far south as York. The Picts would sometimes stage raids just to remind the Romans of their abiding hostility.

Calach led most of the raids on Roman forts. His reputation grew among the Romans and the Britons alike, and they came to dread his arrival.

Melcon died a few years after Agricola's retreat, and the Caledonii chose Gabhran as their new king. Calach served his new king with pride, swearing his life to protect him, and to do his bidding forever.

When Finn, Calach's faithful deer hound, eventually died, Calach felt truly alone with his memories, and with the bitterness that still simmered in his heart. He was sure he would never overcome it.

One day, in Calach's sixty-third year, a frantic Selgovae delegation arrived in Caledonia with news that galvanized the Picts.

The Romans were coming again, in force. A legion had breached the Tweed.

When word reached Calach, he had been in seclusion at his chosen retreat on the remote ridge. He received the news in wordless, distant sadness, and he remained there in thoughtful solitude long after the messenger had left.

Gaius Julius Livius had long anticipated this day. After years of rumors and stories of raiding Picts, Rome wanted its suspicions put to rest. Many suspected, and Livius knew, that the Picts had not truly been vanquished at all at the place called "Mons Graupius', but had rather somehow frightened the legions away. Livius yearned to finish what he knew had not been accomplished. He dreamed of finally crushing the insolent Picts.

Livius led what he imagined to be the finest legion of Rome. Over the decades, it had proven itself in countless campaigns from Britain to the Holy Land, and it was fitting that the Ninth should be chosen to accomplish this special task. The single black mark on its long and distinguished history had come at the hands of these barbarians, in a bloody massacre that no one ever dared to discuss.

Livius well knew of it, though. He knew of his uncle, who had escaped the carnage, much to his undying shame. As the Ninth had been rebuilt, the survivors of the raid had been culled from the Legion, some executed for failure or cowardice, and the rest had been relegated to a life of disgrace and remorse. Livius's mother had told him the tale in hushed tones late at night, as he drifted to sleep, and in that sleep he had dreamed his revenge.

And now he was here to have it. For Livius, his assignment to the resurrected Ninth, and Rome's approval for this campaign, was the fulfillment of his lifelong dream. He marched proudly at the head of his column as it drove into this misty land, which had come to be thought of as haunted and forbidden by the locally garrisoned troops.

After two uneventful weeks of marching in a dark, relentless rain, and making camp in long abandoned garrisons, the Ninth had come to the fort that had existed only in tales. It was the site of that unmentionable shame, the slaughter of the Ninth. As the new Ninth settled in for the night, Livius stood for a very long time in the center of the fort, absorbing the feel and the smell of his surroundings, cursing the rain, and imagining the grim details of what must have happened here that day so long ago. It was late into the night before he turned in for a restless sleep.

Livius awoke groggy, as one does from the deep sleep that finally follows anxious, sleepless hours. His head pounded as he sat up, rubbing his swollen and gritty eyes. He realized that he had been awakened by a sound, and that the sound was coming from the hills surrounding the fort. It was a ghostly, haunting sound, and he knew it had to be the Pictish pipes that he had heard so much about.

"And so it begins," he muttered, as he rose from his bed.

Livius walked toward the opening of his tent wondering how long he had slept, and whether the sun had yet risen above the thick, low clouds that had poured endless, drenching rain throughout the night. He knew he would do battle today, and he hoped that the weather had turned; Livius hated to fight in the rain. He walked through the opening and into the shock of his life.

The man standing just outside his tent was in his sixties, Livius thought, but he was still as strong and forbidding as any barbarian Livius had ever seen. Livius realized while he stared at the man that the fort was filled with strangers, blue-skinned, painted people who were barely clothed and fully armed. He sensed that there was barely room to move. He didn't take his eyes from the older man.

The man was a Pict; that much was clear. His wild hair was matted in the rain, which had not stopped, and it clung to the bluish face that was covered with deeply etched tattoos. The bluish skin accented clear hazel eyes that were filled with an ancient and smoldering hatred. The eyes bore deeply into Livius, and Livius was reluctantly impressed by the power of this man.

Calach stood silent, unmoving, waiting for the Roman legate to comprehend the hopelessness of his situation.

Livius looked around finally, to see what had to be twenty thousand Picts crowded into the fort. The gates stood open, the sentries lying motionless on the ground beside them. Soldiers stood rain-drenched in front of their tents, having been dragged out of their sleep by their captors, who now held them at the points of their swords. Some of the tents were silent; their occupants had been killed in their sleep. The silence that lay over the fort was surreal considering the flurry of activity all around. The Roman soldiers appeared to be in shock.

Calach continued to stare silently at the legate. Livius was stunned by the number of Picts that had crept, apparently noiselessly, into the fort. The pipes droned their mournful sound, and drums began to beat ominously. Livius knew in that moment that all of the Romans would die.

"Who are you?" Livius asked. Calach glared, and after a long moment, he spoke.

"I am Calach," he said.

"Galgacus," Livius said softly, almost in awe, speaking the name the Romans had given him so long ago. Calach snarled. He hated the false name.

"Calach," he hissed emphatically.

"Calach," Livius repeated. It was awkward for him to pronounce. "What do you want from us?" Livius knew as he asked it that the question was absurd. He thought that Calach might laugh. He did not. Instead, he took three menacing steps toward Livius, and Livius expected Calach's sword.

"What I want," said Calach "is what was promised!"

"What was promised?" Livius asked, bewildered. "What do you mean? What promise?"

"The promise that you would never come here. The promise that if you ever did, you would die. I only want what was promised long ago, by your general and by me. Today I will have what was promised." Calach looked around the fort, at the shivering Roman soldiers and at the Picts waiting patiently for Calach's word. His eyes returned to Livius.

"Because you brought them here, for whatever reason you had, your men will all die today. What could you have possibly been thinking?"

"Your defeat is inevitable," Livius said. "It is only a matter of time."

"Perhaps." Calach was circumspect. "But if that day comes, it will not be a day that either you or I will see. We will not be defeated by Rome, and if we are ever defeated, it will be long after Rome has turned to dust. Like Agricola, you live in dreams. Hold your dreams tightly as you die." Calach paused, and then said, "You should not have come here."

Calach motioned to the Picts, and the screams began. Calach stared stoically into Livius's eyes as the second massacre of the Ninth was carried out. None escaped, and none survived. It happened in a matter of minutes, and then the fort fell silent again.

Livius stood pale and shaking, overwhelmed by the magnitude of what he had just seen and heard. His entire life had been taken from him in a moment, and yet he was still alive. He did not know why he was still alive.

"A man just like you stood silent," Calach said, "as his soldiers raped and killed unarmed villagers. The Selgovae were peaceable people. They hurt no one. Those soldiers killed thousands, slowly, enjoying the act. Friends of mine watched, powerless to stop it, and they lived with that for the rest of their lives. You will live with what you have just seen, and were powerless to stop, for the rest of your life. Be thankful that will not be long."

Calach turned and walked away from Livius, and toward the open gates of the fort. As he walked, the Picts began to speak his name.

"Calach! Calach! Calach!"

The chant grew louder, and by the time he got to the gates it resounded through the surrounding hills. He walked through the gates without looking back, and was gone.

As ordered, Ailpein waited for hours while Livius knelt, sobbing, in the mud. As Livius was finally pulled to his feet, his sobbing subsided. He stood hugging himself in the rain as an ancient Selgovae hunter stepped forward to face him.

Livius looked deeply into the Pict's old and anguished eyes. Livius knew that this man had known great pain. For a strange and inexplicable reason, Livius wanted desperately to know the man's name. He could not bring himself to ask it.

"I am Sioltach, the Selgovae warrior," Sioltach said softly, his voice raspy and rough. "I am a Pict. My family is long dead, but I am still alive. I have lived only to see this day."

Sioltach the Selgovae warrior drew his sword. He hesitated for a moment, glaring hard into his enemy's eyes. Suddenly, without another word, Sioltach swung his sword and struck off the Roman's head.

23

Calach and Girom

CALACH SAT COMFORTABLY with his back against a hollow in the trunk of his favorite tree. He looked out over the patchwork of the valley below into his past. He had been coming here since he was a boy, in search of insight, and wisdom, and strength. These days he came here to reminisce.

Today he strained his eyes to see out over the distant mountains. He tried to conjure Fiona's gentle face, and her loving eyes. Sometimes when he sat here deep in thought, he could almost hear her voice whispering to him, comforting him, calling his name.

Calach sensed a presence behind him, and he heard the rustling of leaves and soft footsteps on the sod. He froze, alert.

"Calach…" The voice was old and gravelly, soft and familiar. Calach smiled to himself.

"Girom, is that you?" He knew it was.

"Yes, lad. It is me."

"You must be ancient," Calach exclaimed, as he stood to turn and face Girom. When he saw him, his jaw dropped in dismay. Girom had not aged a day. He looked exactly as he had the first time Calach laid eyes on him decades ago.

"What–," Calach began.

"You're weary, lad," Girom interrupted, with half a smile on his face. "You have seen much since we last spoke."

"How can this be?" Calach asked. "I've aged sixty years, and you have not aged a day." Girom ignored his query.

"You feel your soul is broken, my boy," Girom said. Calach looked away with misty eyes. His jaw tensed as he struggled to maintain his composure. Girom shook his head sadly. "Battered, it is, yes. But not broken. Never broken."

"I have failed," Calach lamented.

Girom stood for a long time gazing out over the valley. Misty clouds were gathering as if conjured from thin air.

"You have failed," Girom finally replied, nodding. He paused for a long moment. Calach was mildly surprised by the response, but then Girom continued. "And you have triumphed. All men fail, and all men triumph. The things that you should be considering are *why* you fought, *how* you fought, and what you did with the triumph or failure you achieved."

"I have failed where I swore to succeed," Calach said.

Girom grinned, and asked, "Did you succeed where you swore to fail?"

Calach was slightly annoyed. *No one swears to fail,* he thought to himself. *This old man has grown foolish.* Calach said nothing.

"Indeed…," Girom said, as if in answer to Calach's thoughts. "No one swears to fail." Girom turned to Calach with a mischievous grin. "Or do they? Perhaps the question is not as foolish as one might think."

Calach flushed in embarrassment.

"Tell me of your failure, Calach," Girom said. "Define it. How have you failed?"

Calach thought carefully as he constructed his answer.

"I was overcome by rage so long ago," Calach said. "It has burned within me for most of my life. I have done violence in the name of vengeance, and I have found gratification in that."

"And that was wrong," Girom said.

"Yes," Calach replied. "I had sworn to be nobler than that."

Girom thought for a moment.

"You raged against the Romans," he finally said, nodding.

"Yes," Calach replied, "I rage against the Romans, and against Brude's betrayal. Against a dozen other wrongs, as well. But mostly I have raged over the loss of my dear Fiona."

Girom nodded his understanding.

"The Romans were evil men," Girom said. "They took from you much."

"Aye," Calach agreed. "Too much."

"Tell me, Calach," Girom said quietly. "The things the Romans did, the things they took from you…was it not in their nature to do such things?"

"I suppose it was," Calach said.

"Is it not, in fact, in the very nature of all men to do such things?"

Calach considered the question. He thought of the Urnifal, and of many others who had attacked the Picts over the centuries.

"I suppose it is in the nature of some men," Calach conceded.

"Perhaps of *most* men?" Girom asked.

"Perhaps."

"When Brude betrayed you to the Romans, were his actions not consistent with human nature?"

Calach nodded. "Yes, I suppose they were," he said.

"Would you say, then, that you have raged mostly against acts of human nature?"

"I suppose I could say that," Calach grudgingly agreed. "But I rage against myself, too – against my failures, against the things that I should have done differently. My blunder cost Fiona her life."

"Your failures and mistakes – are they not the result of your own human nature? When you rage against such things, are you not raging – once again – against human nature…your *own* human nature?" Girom asked.

Calach looked quizzically at Girom.

"You wanted to be nobler than you were," Girom observed.

"I tried so hard," Calach answered.

"And at times you failed," Girom continued. "Which means that there were other times when you did *not* fail? So, in some ways, at some times, you were noble at least to some degree?"

"Perhaps, but not enough."

"Ah, but Calach, don't you see?" Girom sighed. "Nobility is a victory of the spirit over human nature. Such is a rare occurrence in most men's lives, and sometimes a frequent occurrence in rare men's lives."

Calach thought deeply, considering Girom's words.

"You have achieved this more than once, I would suspect," Girom continued.

Calach began to feel an ancient weight lifting from his heavy heart. He began to comprehend Girom's salient point.

"Calach," Girom continued, "listen to me. There are good men, there are bad men, and there are ordinary men."

Calach listened intently.

"Most men simply live according to their human nature," Girom said, "which is a cloak that the spirit accepts when it descends into human form. Ordinary men, by their very nature, are selfish, aggressive, often violent, and occasionally compassionate or kind.

"Bad men, however, are those who have descended to the lowest depths of human nature; they are voracious, cruel, hateful, and destructive. They care for nothing and no one, but for themselves and for whatever they wish to consume.

"Good men, on the other hand, occasionally act in harmony with their spiritual nature, their higher selves. But mostly they wear the cloak of their human nature. Good men almost always fail to be truly, unequivocally noble. But they try, always."

Calach nodded now. He could clearly see Girom's truth.

"To be human," Girom continued, "is not failure, my son. Humanity is a challenge, an opportunity for the spirit to occasionally triumph over the flesh. When men transcend their human nature, they are selfless, forgiving, kind, and noble. A single instance of this in a human lifetime can be considered a tremendous achievement."

"And I have accomplished that," Calach half-questioned, knowing the answer.

"You, Calach, have achieved more than you can imagine, much more than you have allowed yourself to see. You've been too consumed with chastising your humanity. Your self-reproach is itself a spiritual act, an act of strength, and of purity of heart."

"So," Calach said, "I have not truly failed." Calach was pleased with that conclusion.

"You have failed," Girom assured him.

Calach frowned, perturbed. Girom seemed to be toying with him.

"And you have triumphed," Girom added, smiling widely.

Calach's frown broke into a grin.

"You, my friend, should be celebrating your spirit, which has guided you relentlessly in spite of your many lapses into human nature." Almost as an afterthought, he added, "Your triumphs over human nature have been many, my noble friend."

"It was easy to be noble and strong," Calach said, "until they took away the one thing I loved more than life itself. They took my Fiona, the love of my life. She was my breath–"

"They took nothing," Girom interrupted. He placed his arm around Calach's shoulders. "Look into the gathering mist, young Calach. Look long and hard and you will see that your Fiona awaits you." Girom pointed with an outstretched hand, his fingers long and bony and bluish, toward the mountains.

Calach looked first into Girom's kind, soulful eyes, and then toward the mountains in the distance.

"She never left you," Girom continued. "She has always been with you, whispering to you, pointing out the path that you should follow. She rejoiced when you heard her whisper, and she understood when you did not. She has watched your efforts and your progress with a joyful heart filled with admiration and love."

"My progress," Calach mused. "All this time I felt that I had failed tragically."

"It is difficult to see clearly in the darkness of this world," Girom said. "Only when your soul is freed of its earthly bond are you able to accurately assess your losses and your triumphs. Only then will you fully realize that in many of your losses you have gained, while in many of your triumphs you have lost much.

"You will then see clearly that you lived better than most, that there is much for which you can be proud. You will see that you have truly lived this life well, Calach."

"Free of its earthly bond?" Calach repeated.

"Cruithne left this world with many of the same thoughts with which you struggle now," Girom said. "He felt he had failed, because he fell short of his own expectations."

"Cruithne? How could that be so? He was the greatest hero!"

"In the spirit world, after he had passed on and was free of his earthly shell, he saw clearly that he had accomplished what he had come to accomplish. He had overcome his fear of the unknown. He found the courage to turn from battle and save a nation. He lived in purity and strength, so that his life has been remembered to this day. You are a testament to that."

"And yet he felt that he had failed..."

"Yes...you felt that you had failed...much as you do now."

Calach's face clouded with confusion. He searched Girom's eyes.

"You feel that way again..." Girom repeated, looking intently at Calach.

"Again..." Calach returned Girom's gaze.

"Your spirit is strong, my son," Girom soothed, "and brave. You have lived well, yet again. You took upon yourself a heavy burden so long ago, as Cruithne. It was a burden under which almost any man would have been crushed. You reproved yourself then, as you do now, for your failure to meet your own expectations."

"Cruithne..." Calach repeated, placing a trembling hand to his own chest.

"Cruithne," Girom nodded, smiling.

"Then it's true..."

"It is true."

Calach thought deeply, and for a very long time.

"And I will return, yet again?"

"Yet again," Girom confirmed.

Calach trembled visibly as he formed his next question.

"Fiona?" he asked.

Girom gazed long into the distance. A smile tugged at the corners of his mouth, and his eyes sparkled like brilliant, blazing diamonds. He took a very deep breath, and then he nodded slowly and ever so slightly.

"Aye...," the old man breathed.

Author's Note

The Picts of the Dark Ages were a mysterious and reclusive people, about whom little history of any veracity has ever been recorded. They appear to have wished for their existence to remain obscure, both from their contemporaries and from posterity. They eagerly sought the seclusion of the virtually impenetrable Scottish highlands. The only written document the Picts left for future historians is a simple list of their kings spanning a relatively short period of their history, from AD 388 to 842.

The only existing insight into the origins, the language, the customs, and the nature of the elusive and enigmatic Picts is found in the disputable documentation of a personally motivated Roman historian, and in meager evidence uncovered by the few archaeologists who have worked diligently to uncover and analyze relics of their civilization. The absence of credible historical records and the scarcity of archaeological evidence leave us only with supposition and conjecture about the Picts. Even the origin of their name is widely debated among historians.

What we do know for certain is that the Picts existed, and that they lived in what is now Scotland, north of the Tweed River. We also know that the Romans never succeeded in subjugating them. There is no evidence to suggest that any other army ever conquered them, either.

The only recorded history of Rome's encounters with the Picts was published by Gaius Cornelius Tacitus, the son-in-law of the general Agricola. According to Tacitus, Agricola successfully led the conquest and subjugation of the Picts in AD 84. Tacitus was clearly and considerably motivated to present Agricola's accomplishments favorably, and there were few who possessed the resources or the motivation to prove or to refute his published accounts. His accounts are therefore likely to be, at least to some degree, embellished or contrived.

What is beyond debate is that the Roman Empire never extended into Pictish lands. Maps of the Roman Empire at its zenith make that clear. In spite of the considerable resources the Romans dedicated to the conquest of the entire island of Britannia, they failed to accomplish that imperative goal.

Hadrian's Wall, the Antonine Wall, and the firmly established southern Scottish border have remained as firm testimony of the Romans' inability to triumph over Pictish resilience. Subsequent Scottish history shows clearly that the Picts remained intact, and increasingly united, for at least four hundred years after the Roman Empire disintegrated.

The Picts, despite relentless outside pressure, remained throughout their history an unvanquished civilization. In the end, the Picts' custom of matrilineal inheritance and their extensive intermarriage with the Scots led to their assimilation into the kingdom of the Scots, who were the last to try – and to fail – to conquer them militarily.

Kenneth MacAlpin, a Scot, was the first to hold dual kingship over both the Scots and the Picts. His mother was a Pictish princess, and his father was Alpin, King of Scots. His father was captured and beheaded by the Picts in his final attempt to conquer them. MacAlpin avenged his father by initiating the assimilation of the Picts into the Scottish kingdom. While it took more than four hundred years, the Scottish culture ultimately absorbed and suppressed the indomitable kingdom of the Picts.

The Pict is the story of Calach, one of the most accomplished, elusive, and mysterious of Pictish heroes, who lived centuries before the Scots began to arrive in numbers from Ireland. Calach inspired a loose affiliation of Pictish tribes to unite and to successfully defy an onslaught of invading Roman legions, and to begin their evolution into a cohesive and dominant culture.

Calach's words in this novel's account of his meeting with Agricola are loosely based upon a speech attributed to Galgacus in *The Life of Gnaeus Julius Agricola*, written by Tacitus (Agricola's son-in-law) in AD 98, and translated by Alfred John Church and William Jackson Brodribb. Tacitus's account of Galgacus's speech to his army at the start of the fabled battle at Mons Graupius appears to be largely embellished, if not wholly fictitious. It is unlikely that any Roman was close enough to Galgacus to hear him, or fast enough with a pen to record, or capable of remembering verbatim the speech of nearly 1,000 words that Galgacus is supposed to have made to his warriors, who would have been waiting impatiently for battle.

But it is clear that Calach was one of many who through the ages established and defended the unyielding southern border of the Pictish, and later the Scottish domain.

The Picts did not cease to exist. Pictish blood flows through the hearts of modern day Scots, who retain the same notions of freedom and honor that motivated the Picts so long ago to defend themselves against the multitude of Roman legions.

Calach's spirit, likewise, lives on.

A majority of the world's population believes in the immortality of the human soul. A smaller majority also believes in reincarnation. If that particular belief has merit, then Calach's soul, along with those of the people with whom he experienced his life, may have returned to experience the drama of other lives, in other places and in other times, shaping and reshaping the world into which we are born, and reborn, learning from a succession of failure and success, triumph and loss, elation and inestimable grief. Calach's story is but one of many, each noteworthy and unique in its contribution to the continuing story of man, and each with a message for our own dramatic and challenging lives.

Calach's story is but one of many yet to come.

Contact the author at his web site: www.jdixon.net

978-0-981-76712-3
0-981-76712-5

9497954R0

Made in the USA
Lexington, KY
02 May 2011